The
Ghost of
Gosswater

Lucy
Strange

Chicken
House

2 Palme

Text © Lucy Strange 2020

First published in Great Britain in 2020
Chicken House
2 Palmer Street
Frome, Somerset BA11 1DS
United Kingdom
www.chickenhousebooks.com

Cover and interior design by Helen Crawford-White
Typeset by Dorchester Typesetting Group Ltd
Printed and bound in Great Britain by CPI Group (UK) Ltd, Croydon CR0 4YY

The paper used in this Chicken House book is made from
wood grown in sustainable forests.

3 5 7 9 10 8 6 4 2

British Library Cataloguing in Publication data available.

PB ISBN 978-1-911077-84-8
eISBN 978-1-913322-61-8

For Fred

In Aeternum Fidelis

We know what we are,
but know not what we may be.

Ophelia

WILLIAM SHAKESPEARE, *HAMLET*

The Lake District, England
1899

I

A cold, wet morning – 21st December 1899

Father died last night, and now here we are, eating breakfast as if everything were perfectly normal.

'Pass me the butter will you, dearest Agatha?' Cousin Clarence asks.

I look at him for a moment, then I stand up and walk the length of the dining table and deposit the butter dish with a clatter. My cousin doesn't flinch, but his enormous dog growls at me from beneath the tablecloth.

'Good boy, Brutus,' Clarence chuckles, slipping a sausage under the table. I try to ignore the monstrous snapping and gobbling sound.

Clarence waits for me to walk all the way back to my chair and sit down again before he adds, 'And the salt?'

Wilson, the butler, is hovering by the door. He shuffles towards the table, but Clarence waves him away. 'Don't worry, Wilkins.'

'Wilson, sir.'

'My young cousin likes to make herself useful. Don't you, Agatha? No need for you to hang about, Wilkins.'

Wilson sniffs and leaves the room, and I take Clarence the salt. I make sure my face is blank, giving no hint of the hot hatred stirring within me. I refuse to give him the satisfaction. Clarence has been like this since he arrived at Gosswater Hall two weeks ago – playful, cruel – like a cat with a sparrow between its paws. No sooner had the doctor declared that Father was 'nearing the end' than Cousin Clarence appeared at the door, with his slobbering dog and his crocodile smile. Clarence is the heir to the Gosswater estate. He has reminded me of this every single day he has been here. And now that Father has died, Cousin Clarence is the new Earl of Gosswater.

He doesn't look anything like an earl.

I watch him tossing the blond forelock from his eyes, spearing a sausage and stuffing it into his loose-lipped mouth. There is nothing even vaguely noble about Clarence's posture, his manner. He's more animal than aristocrat.

Brutus emerges from beneath the table, his huge head and shoulders dragging at the tablecloth and jangling the china. He is disgusting – all lolling tongue and dripping jowls. Father always said that animals belong outdoors – so the only dogs I have ever seen are sheepdogs and hunting hounds, and always at a distance. Brutus lumbers towards me, and I freeze.

'Don't worry, little cousin,' Clarence grins. 'He's just after your breakfast.'

'Well, he can't have it.' I shove the last bit of buttered crumpet in my mouth.

Brutus stops and growls.

I growl back.

He snarls, his quivering lip lifting to reveal a set of pointed yellow fangs. He steps forward and I feel a quick dart of fear in my stomach. I force myself to look away from the hideous beast and fix my gaze on my hideous cousin instead. I chew my cold crumpet. I hope Clarence can tell how much I hate him.

He meets my gaze and smiles slowly. He's building up to an announcement – I can see it in the smug arrangement of his face. 'You can't stay here, I'm afraid, Agatha,' he declares.

At first I think he means here at the table, but after a moment I realize he means here at Gosswater Hall. I put down my teacup. '*I can't stay here?*'

Clarence devours a forkful of sausage. Brutus goes back to sit by his master's side and is rewarded with a slice of black pudding. Clarence fusses the horrid creature's floppy ears.

He has not answered my question. He is taking his time. He is enjoying this.

'What do you *mean*, I can't stay here, Clarence?'

He looks up again, that smile still on his face. 'Gosswater Hall is mine now, Agatha. You'll be leaving tomorrow.'

Leaving?

'What are you talking about, Clarence? This is my *home*. I thought . . .'

'What did you *think*?' He waves his fork about. 'That I would want my twelve-year-old cousin living here with me, like some sort of annoying pet?'

Brutus snaps his slobbery jaws — *that* position is already taken.

Leave Gosswater Hall? I don't know what to say. Something inside me is unravelling like wool. First Father's death and now this . . . Gosswater Hall is the only home I have ever known, and I can count on my fingers and toes the number of times I've gone beyond the walls of the estate; Mother and Father rarely allowed it.

Clarence hunches like a vulture, and grins at me from beneath his hooded eyes: there is no kindness there, no mercy. 'I'm sorry to have to break this to you, Cousin Agatha . . .'

He doesn't look sorry at all.

'But there's another bit of bad news.' He reaches into his jacket pocket and pulls out an important-looking document. The wax seal has been broken. As Clarence unfolds the papers – deliberately slowly – I glimpse the Asquith family crest at the top of the first page.

Father's will – it has to be . . .

Clarence licks his lips as they twitch into another smile. 'It turns out, Agatha, that the earl and countess were *not* actually your real parents. We already knew, of course, that the Gosswater estate would be passing to me, as the rightful male heir, but this news – *this* news – means that you, my dearest cousin, are not legally entitled to anything *at all*! Nothing in trust, no annuity, not a penny!'

He waits for me to say something, but my voice has stopped working. My throat is dry and tight. I can feel my heart beating in the tips of my fingers.

He holds the paper up for me to see – as if I can read it from this distance. 'Just to be clear, dear Agatha – this document declares that you are illegitimate. You are nobody.' He grins. 'And you're leaving tomorrow. As a matter of fact . . .' He pauses again, relishing the drama of the moment. 'I have arranged for you to be collected from Gosswater Hall by your real father.'

The shock is so great that, at first, I just stare at him dumbly. It is as if he has shot me with a pistol: BANG. At first – nothing – but then, very slowly, the pain spreads. *My real father? What is he talking about?*

Clarence wipes his greasy face with his napkin, flourishes the will triumphantly as he stands up, and then tucks it back safely in his jacket pocket. He slaps his leg to summon Brutus, and the pair of them leave the room in a sort of gloating, prancing parade.

If I could, I would hurl the silver pepper pot after them, but the impulse gets stuck somewhere inside me and my arm doesn't move. I am left alone at the table, with the empty plates and the cold tea, and the knowledge that I am no longer Lady Agatha Asquith of Gosswater – and I never really have been. According to Cousin Clarence, I now have no home, no family, no money, no title . . .

And tomorrow, I am to be given away to a perfect stranger.

2

I spend the rest of the day packing my things, dazed, drugged, with the confusion of it all.

This can't be real, Agatha, my brain says. *There must have been a mistake. Surely, something will happen to stop it . . .* But the hours slide by and nothing happens to stop it, and my hands keep folding my clothes as if they have resigned themselves to this ridiculous fate.

I make a pile of my favourite books – some Dickens, Robert Louis Stevenson, the Brontës, my *Complete Works of Shakespeare* with the thin gold ribbon marking my place in *Hamlet*. I find my needlework bag with its half-finished sampler depicting the Asquith family crest. I throw the sampler on the fire, but change my mind immediately and whip it off the coals before it catches. I brush it clean, roll it up again and put it back in the bag to take with me. *You're not giving up, Agatha,* my brain says. *Even if you do have to leave Gosswater Hall tomorrow, it won't be for ever. It* can't *be . . .*

The housekeeper, Miss McCarthy, helps me to pack my books and clothes into the travelling trunk. I go to the large wardrobe and pull out two of my best silk dresses.

'Not those ones, Agatha, love,' Miss McCarthy says gently. 'His Lordship said the most expensive dresses should stay here.' She sees the expression on my face change. 'Ah now, I'm sorry.'

'Not even one silk dress?'

She hesitates. 'Well, what the eye doesn't see . . . Maybe just one.'

I take the blue.

'Sure, that one suits you so well. Perhaps you could wear it tomorrow?'

'Perhaps.'

Miss McCarthy puts her arm around my shoulders and squeezes me. 'It can't be helped,' she says. 'And what can't be helped must be borne.'

How can she be so docile about this? So accepting? I shrug her off. Miss McCarthy has looked after me since I was a baby. She has been more than just a house-keeper – she has been my ally, my protector. Why isn't she protecting me now? Why isn't she fighting for me?

'Tell him!' I snap. 'Go and tell Clarence that it's all nonsense – that this is my *home*.'

Miss McCarthy just shakes her head. She dabs at her eyes with a handkerchief. 'It can't be helped,' she says again. 'It will be all right, Agatha love. It will all be all right – I promise you.'

But how can she possibly promise me that?

After lunch, Miss McCarthy is ordered to go to her quarters to pack her own bags. I hear one maid whisper to another in the corridor that Clarence is having 'a clean sweep'. Wilson, the butler, has been dismissed too, along with Father's valet and both footmen. They are being taken to the train station at Penrith, and Miss McCarthy is to return to her family in Ireland. The wool unravels further – everything is coming undone. Something inside my chest aches unbearably when I think of those last moments with Miss McCarthy – how I couldn't return her embrace; how I dismissed her from my room as if she were nothing more than a scullery maid.

My hands are shaking so much that I can't fold the nightgown I am holding. What am I afraid of? Everything. Suddenly I am afraid of *everything*, because everything is changing all at once.

I sit down on the bed and smooth the embroidered counterpane with trembling fingers. My heart flickers in my chest like a wind-blown flame. This room has been my cocoon: I could shut the door, and shut out the loneliness. *Choosing* to be alone – that is something quite different. I have learnt that if you choose to be alone, the coldness of others cannot touch you. I would light the fire, and curl up on the window seat with my book. I would gaze out at Lake Gosswater and the distant fells – always the same view – the colours burning and fading with the changing seasons: a perfectly framed picture.

I look around and say goodbye to a room that already feels as if it belongs to someone else. Even the pattern of the wallpaper seems unfamiliar – the geese in flight embossed upon the silk blue sky. *Where are they flying to?* I wonder, and the ache in my chest gets worse . . . *Where am I flying to?*

Unable to bear the strangeness of it all, I find myself drifting up the stairs to my old nursery on the top floor. I put my hands down on the steps in front of me and climb up on all fours – like I used to when I was small. The wood beneath my hands is gritty with dust and dirt.

I haven't been in here for months. When I turned twelve, Mother and Father decided I was too old for a nanny and they never got around to hiring a governess. I found it eerie, being up here alone – the echo of my own voice; the tea set laid out for guests who would never come; the staring eyes of the china dolls.

The air behind the heavy door is cold and musty. It is like stepping into a tomb. There are footsteps thumping up the stairs behind me, and a shadow falls across the dusty floorboards.

'Come to say bye-bye to your dollies, have you, Agatha?' Clarence barges into the room. 'Oh, yes – a fine nursery. And look – a tea party all ready for me. How jolly!'

He picks up one of my old dolls. I feel an angry, possessive pang. 'That's mine,' I say, striding over and snatching it to my chest.

There's a low growl right behind me and I spin around to see Brutus – teeth bared and muzzle drooling. My heart jumps – I didn't hear him come in. He pads to Clarence's side and I keep my eyes on him as I move back towards the staircase. I just wanted a moment alone up here, but Clarence has ruined it. He has ruined everything.

'Oh – look at this chap!' Clarence exclaims, approaching my old rocking horse and patting his grey-painted neck. 'You need a bit of sprucing up, old fellow, but you're well made. Yes – you'll do very nicely for the next generation of Asquiths.'

My fingers grip the door frame. 'The next generation, Clarence?'

He smiles a coy smile. 'Well. Not for a year or two, perhaps, but I'm sure it won't be long . . .'

I sway slightly, sickened at the thought of Clarence's vile offspring clambering and dribbling all over my rocking horse.

Clarence swings a tight-trousered leg and deposits

his substantial weight on the poor horse's back. The old wood creaks. He gathers up the red reins and sets off at a rolling canter. 'I, Clarence Mallory Asquith, Thirtieth Earl of Gosswater, am now the wealthiest and most eligible bachelor in all of Cumberland! In the whole of England, I should think!' He whips at the rocking horse's flank and halloos his imaginary hunt: 'TALLY-HO, my fine beauties!'

Brutus joins in the madness, leaping and barking with excitement. He starts sniffing about frantically, as if there are foxes hiding in the shadowed corners of the nursery. Clarence laughs loudly. 'Sniff 'em out, boy – sniff 'em out!'

I can't stand it. 'This is a house of mourning, Clarence,' I say, raising my voice above their mayhem. 'Where is your *respect*?'

Clarence guffaws again. 'I'm the Earl of Gosswater, Agatha, and this is *my* house – I can do WHATEVER I LIKE!'

You can't let him win this easily, Agatha, my brain hisses.

I feel myself flushing with anger. But what can I say? What can I do? I turn back to the dark staircase in defeat. Clarence's voice pursues me down to the floor below: 'TALLY-HOOOO!' Another flight, two floors down . . . As the sound fades, my anger begins to fade too. Something else takes its place – a colder, calmer feeling, diamond-hard. Another flight down and I am in the eye of the storm – anger, grief, fear and confusion are whirling around me, but here in the centre I am able to think perfectly clearly. By the time I reach the landing overlooking the atrium, I have made an important decision.

I am going to *take* something.

I am entitled to more than just a few books, some clothes and this dusty old doll in my hand. No matter what Clarence says, I refuse to be 'nothing', and I have no intention of walking away from Gosswater Hall without taking something valuable with me.

I will take the King Stone.

I allow myself a private smile. Without the King Stone, dear Cousin Clarence will find that he is significantly less 'eligible' than he first thought.

3

There it is, mounted within the huge carved shield above the stairs – dark and gleaming, like the eye of a giant raven. The King Stone is the biggest black opal in the world. Clarence bought it last year, once he knew that he would soon become the Thirtieth Earl. He had it cut to match the exact proportions of the original jewel of Gosswater – the Queen Stone – a legendary white opal that had been in the Asquith family for centuries.

Hundreds of years ago, all the landowners in the kingdom were asked to send gifts of food and wine to celebrate the king's marriage, but the young Lord Asquith's crops had failed so all he was able to send was a single egg from his flock of geese that grazed on the banks of Lake Gosswater. During the king's wedding banquet, an army of rebels attacked the castle with the intention of killing the king and kidnapping the new queen. The king and his men were all unarmed, and defeat looked certain until something extraordinary happened. Asquith's goose egg hatched, and from it there flew a hundred fierce, fully grown geese, who chased the rebels away. In gratitude, the king made Asquith an earl. He gave him the Gosswater estate and the new queen sent him her greatest jewel – a white opal as big as a goose egg. From that day, the Queen Stone was the symbol of the Asquith family's noble lineage and our loyalty to the crown. But this stone disappeared years ago – it went missing before I was born.

Cousin Clarence clearly felt that he couldn't be a proper earl without a proper jewel, and, in the absence of the Queen Stone, he produced the *King* Stone.

As if you can buy nobility, my brain scoffs.

I don't know if he intended to get a black opal instead of a white one, or if it was just a stupid mistake (probably the latter, knowing Clarence). It makes me think of the marble chess set in Father's study – the white queen versus the black king . . .

Checkmate, Clarence, I smile to myself as I reach up to take the King Stone from its mount within the shield. But then there is a noise from below. I peer over the balustrade, down into the great hallway that Father always insisted on calling 'the atrium', and see a group

17

of workmen trooping through the front door. A maid runs to meet them, flapping and twittering – they really *must* use the door by the kitchens. The workmen are talking about ladders and chandeliers. They have come to refurbish the ballroom for the new earl.

The ballroom? When did Clarence organize this? Father hasn't even been buried yet . . .

Then the maid comes running up the stairs towards me.

I move away from the shield, trying to make it look as if I am merely studying the carvings on the oak balustrade. Woven about the twining branches and twisting ivy of the original work, are motifs added by a more modern craftsman – owls, wrens, hedgehogs, butterflies. My fingertips trace the shape of a fox hidden amongst the leaves.

The maid bobs a curtsey as she dashes past.

One of the workmen looks up at me from the atrium and doffs his cap politely.

This is not the right moment to take the King Stone. Someone will see me.

I will come back for it tonight.

I wait until the house is quiet – the last footsteps of the remaining servants creaking their way up to the attic rooms. Then I get out of bed and go to the door, a candle-holder in my hand. I hear the distant striking of a clock – twelve chimes echo through the night . . .

And then the corridor is silent once more, dwindling to darkness in both directions like an underground tunnel. Instead of heading straight for the stairs, though, I find myself turning towards the Long Gallery. I stop immediately. What has come over me? The Long Gallery is out of bounds. Why on earth would I want to go there alone in the middle of the night? Why would I want to see all those gory paintings and hollow suits of armour by candlelight? But something is drawing me towards it – a soft voice inside my head, crooning and calling to me . . . My feet take another step.

Agatha! my brain hisses. *The King Stone.*

I blink.

The soft, crooning voice has gone.

You imagined it, Agatha. You're dreaming.

I take a long breath, turn around and tiptoe along the corridor. I creep past the Red Room and the Duchess Suite – avoiding the eyes of the ghoulish portrait that hangs on the wall here. My candle flickers in a cold draught and shadows dart about me like dark, feathered things.

I stop outside Father's room. He's still in there, lying on his bed. I hold my breath and listen, but I don't know what I expect to hear. The heavy oak door is shut, and behind it there is only the stillness of the dead. I try not to think about last night, but the dreadful memory worms its way to the forefront of my mind — Father's thin white face beaded with sweat; his thin white hair sticking wetly to the satin pillowcase; his hand gripping mine as he opened his lips to speak, and muttered those incomprehensible last words . . . I could only watch as the last agonizing breaths rattled through his body. The doctor felt his wrist for a pulse and then shook his head.

I stare into the heart of the candle flame, hoping its brightness will burn the memory away.

There was something different about Father in his final days — when he looked at me, his watery old eyes were full of apologies. Perhaps he knew my life was about to be turned upside down. Perhaps he was just sorry he hadn't been kinder . . .

He is gone now, Agatha, my brain whispers.

Yes, he is gone. He is nothing but an empty old shell, waiting in there for the undertakers to collect him. We are both to be collected by strangers tomorrow, Father and I; both to be carted off as if we are merely things cluttering up Clarence's new life. Anger rises in my throat like bile, but it is better than the confusion of feelings I felt just a moment before. It helps me to move forward — away from the door of Father's room and towards the main staircase. My bare feet are silent on the polished steps as I make my way down to the landing. There is a table of ornaments in the alcove here — familiar objects, but somehow strange in the candlelight: a Japanese vase, an Arabian dagger, a brass hunting horn, the skull of a monkey, a cigar bowl blown from black glass . . .

A black glass bowl? It is as if I am suddenly, fully awake. My fingers close around the bowl. *Yes, yes — it's perfect.* I go straight to the carved shield in the middle of the landing and hold my candle up to illuminate the King Stone. The black opal flashes with peacock-green flames. I stand on tiptoe, reach up with trembling fingers and gently lift it from its cup-shaped mount. Then I turn the black glass bowl on its side and wedge it firmly in the King Stone's place. It will take days for Clarence to notice the opal is missing. 'Ha!' I almost jump at the sound of my own laughter. I feel manic, peculiar. Is this who I am now? A trickster? A thief?

You're not a thief, Agatha, my brain says firmly. *It's Clarence who has stolen everything from* you, *remember?*

I cup the opal in my palm, cool and heavy and beautiful.

I am *not* a thief. I am Lady Agatha Asquith of Gosswater, and the King Stone is my rightful inheritance.

4

I am waiting for the man who claims to be my real father. All day, I have been sitting here in the atrium, anxiously sweating into the stiffness of my blue silk dress, with my bags and cases arranged about me. With each hour that passes I grow more and more furious. How *dare* he keep me waiting like this? As the clock strikes four, I decide that the whole thing must be some sort of cruel prank on Clarence's part, but then I hear the sound of a horse and carriage approaching the house. I stand up and go straight to the front door.

Oh – it isn't a horse and carriage; it is a pony and cart. It must be a delivery for the kitchens. I watch as the black pony trots around the curve of the driveway, skirting the dark moat that surrounds the house. It stamps to a halt on the other side of the bridge that leads to the front terrace, and a man climbs down from the cart – a tall man with thick, dark hair. By his clothes, I would say he is a farm worker from the estate – a pigman, perhaps. What is a pigman doing at the front door of the house? I hope he moves his cart before my so-called father arrives. The man stops and turns, looking up at Gosswater Hall in the damp evening gloom. Then he sees me here, standing on the terrace at the top of the steps, and he just stares. Why is he looking at me like that?

I go cold.

No. He can't possibly be . . .

Cousin Clarence comes around the side of the house from the gardens. He practically skips towards the stranger, barely able to conceal his excitement – and that's when I know. *It's him.* This dishevelled visitor is not here on estate business, and he is not making a delivery to the kitchens. He is, supposedly, my real father.

My stomach clenches. I want to run away. I want to scurry up to my bedroom and lock the door. I want to scream into the blackening sky – NO, YOU CAN'T MAKE ME GO! But I don't run, and I don't scream; something else is in control of me now – fate, perhaps? It is dragging me into the next awful moment, unstoppable as a rising tide. I pick up my coat, put it on over my blue dress and do up the buttons with numbed fingers.

Clarence and the man are talking together. I can't hear what they are saying. Clarence is nodding and smiling, his mouth open and tight like an eager dog. The stranger is not smiling at all. Eventually, Clarence comes trotting up the steps on to the marble terrace. 'Well, little cousin,' he pants. 'Are you ready to go?' He places a hand on my shoulder and I stiffen. There is no warmth in his gesture – it is the way you might place a hand on a horse to stop it shying from the bridle.

Don't let him think he's beaten you, Agatha, my brain whispers. *He can't take your whole life away just like that. This isn't the end . . .*

'Yes, I'm ready, Clarence,' I manage to say.

We stand aside as a maid and a boot boy carry my bags and cases over the bridge and the stranger loads them into the cart. Somehow, I keep my voice steady as I lie through my teeth: 'And I must say, I think he looks like a very nice man.'

'Nice?' Clarence raises his pale eyebrows. Then he bends down close to my ear, and I hear the click of spittle as his lips part into a smile. 'Oh, no, he isn't *nice*, Agatha. Thomas Walters is nothing more than a common thief.'

His words flash through me, cold and hot. 'A thief? Clarence, what do you—'

'Cheerio, Agatha!' Clarence interrupts gleefully. He

feigns an avuncular hug, then he pats me so hard on the back that I stumble down the steps, my insides lurching at the sudden sense of falling uncontrollably. I gather my dignity together and look straight ahead – Thomas Walters and his cart are silhouettes in the growing darkness. There is no going back now. This is how a prisoner must feel on their way to the gallows. I put one foot in front of the other, over the bridge, and across the short stretch of driveway to the cart.

The man called Thomas Walters offers his hand to help me up, and I very nearly take it, but then I stop myself. It isn't just because his hand is dirty and I am worried about my only good dress – there are other reasons too. He is a complete stranger, and he is – apparently – a thief. To accept this man's hand would be to accept him as my father, and I am not prepared to do that.

I manage to climb up by myself.

Thomas Walter's hand drops back to his side; the friendly smile dies on his lips.

I know I have been rude, but I am not going to apologize. He has not apologized for keeping me waiting all day. And now he is up on the cart beside me, and the pony is trotting, and he is taking me away from Gosswater Hall to my new home. *His* home.

We rattle down the driveway, the high, hard cart wheels jerking and splashing through the puddled ruts. The black pony puts its head down and trots faster, leaning into the wind. My heart is thudding almost as rapidly as his hooves.

As we approach the iron gates, I turn to look back at the house I have lived in for my entire life, but the dark magic of twilight makes it unfamiliar – a cold, imposing structure of high walls, gloomy towers and gothic turrets. The dregs of the winter sunset are reflected in the round nursery windows on the top floor; they flash like copper coins on the eyelids of the dead. And then we are through the gates and out on to the road, and Gosswater Hall has disappeared from sight. *Will I ever see it again?*

Thomas Walters sits up very straight beside me, and keeps his eyes on the dim road ahead. I look at him from the corner of my eye. He has a long, straight nose; a strong brow bone; a finely angled jaw. His dark eyelashes are long, like a girl's – like mine. Perhaps he really is my father, I think, for a brief, dizzy moment, and instantly dismiss the idea – *How could he possibly be?* My brain is struggling to catch up with everything that is happening. It is half a mile behind us at least, whirling helplessly through dirt and water.

I look at the man's hands again as they grip the wet reins. They are the sort of hands that will never be clean, no matter how much you scrub them. He glances this way – did he notice me looking at him like that? Something about his face looks even darker now – his brow lower, more surly – almost as if he can read my thoughts. What sort of man is he? And where is he taking me? I try to ignore the panic that is advancing through my body like a fever. The further we go from Gosswater Hall, the worse it gets. Are we going far? Will we be travelling all night?

It starts to rain. Instinctively, I arrange my coat so that it covers more of my dress, but the blue silk skirts are wet and dirty already. Oh – my lovely dress! I try to distract myself by concentrating on where we are going. This road is vaguely familiar – I think it leads to Gosswater village, but I can't be sure . . . We are still quite close to the lake. I squint at the wet farmland as we bump and clatter through the downpour: wet sheep, wet fields, wet stone walls. I huddle down into my fur collar. Wherever we are going, I know it will not be as grand as Gosswater Hall. I try to imagine life without servants – no maid to bring my breakfast, no housekeeper, no butler, no boot boy.

'Do you live on a farm?' I ask. It is the first thing either of us has said.

Thomas Walters raises his eyebrows, but he doesn't look at me.

'A farm,' I say again, louder than the running of the wheels and the hiss of the rain. 'Do you live on a farm?'

He jerks his head slightly.

Does that mean yes? It must do. After all, there's nothing else around Gosswater – only farms. And most of them are owned by Father . . .

I blink. No — that's wrong. Everything is different now.

I attempt to rewrite my whole world.

Most of the farms around here were owned by the late Earl of Gosswater, the man I previously believed to be my father . . .

5

Waiting for the journey to be over is like waiting to wake up from a bad dream. I shrink down into my coat and watch the dark, miserable fields spin by.

When we arrive at Thomas Walters' house, I see that it isn't really a house at all – it's a cottage. I've been in a cottage once before: it had low, damp ceilings and smelt of wood smoke. This cottage is about the same size as the gate lodge at Gosswater Hall, but it is built of a lighter coloured stone – just a pale, square shape in the twilight, with latticed windows, a bowed roof and a crooked chimney.

I stare at that chimney. I'm sure I've seen it before . . .

Yes! my brain exclaims. It has caught up with us at

last – thank goodness. It shakes the rain from itself like a wet dog. *We're at that funny cottage perched on the eastern bank of the lake.*

Oh – the relief! It may have felt as if the journey went on for ever, but we can only have travelled a few miles from Gosswater Hall.

I've seen this cottage from the opposite side of Gosswater. On my twelfth birthday, Miss McCarthy took me out for a rare treat: afternoon tea at the Goss Falls Hotel. I remember her pointing out the cottage with the funny chimney: we looked at it through the penny telescope on the hotel terrace. And now that same cottage is to be my new home. *How peculiar . . .*

Thomas has jumped off the cart. He is unbuckling the pony's harness and leading him into a stable: 'Come along, then, George, old boy. Let's get you some hay, shall we?' His voice is low and gentle. George whinnies softly in reply. I hear the jingle of tack being hung on a peg and a hiss-hiss as the pony is vigorously brushed down. There are other sounds too, and I think they are coming from behind the cottage – a rustling, flapping, chattering noise. *Ducks, perhaps?*

Thomas comes out of the stable and goes straight to the front door. He opens it and goes inside. It is dark in there, but he is lighting the lamps and soon the room glows honey-gold through the latticed windows. Smoke rises from the crooked chimney.

I want to go inside, out of the rain, but I don't want

to leave my bags here in the cart. All my things will be ruined.

'Are you goin' to sit out there all night?' Thomas calls from the door. And now I know I have offended him. These are the first words he has spoken to me, and his tone is so different from when he spoke to the pony. He comes out into the yard: 'What are you waitin' for?' There is a note of challenge in his voice now. 'Those bags aren't goin' to bring themselves in.'

I turn and look at the stack of cases and bags in the cart behind me. Surely he doesn't expect *me* to . . .

He is saying he is not your servant, Agatha, my brain says – *however lowly you may think him. He thinks you are a spoilt little miss who has never lifted a finger in her life.*

Defiance hardens inside me and I jump down into the yard, ignoring the freezing water that splashes my stockings. I heave the first case from the cart with no trouble at all, but then struggle to move the big, brass-handled trunk. Thomas is watching me; I am determined to shift it on my own.

'Would you like me to help you with that?' he offers.

I swallow my pride, but it takes some chewing. 'Yes,' I say at last, refusing to look at him.

Thomas doesn't move. I turn around. His arms are folded. He raises his eyebrows as if he is waiting for something.

'Yes. *Please*,' I manage.

Thomas lifts the trunk down as easily as if it were empty, then he leads the way into the cottage. The front door opens straight into a small, bright parlour where a good fire is already crackling away. A steep, narrow staircase is ahead of us. Thomas goes up the stairs, taking care not to scrape the trunk against the wall as he turns the tight corner, down a short landing and into a bedroom no bigger than the meat larder at Gosswater Hall – though I have to say it is a good deal warmer. 'It's not much,' he says, putting down the trunk. 'Not what you're used to, I know. But it'll have to do.' He closes the curtains against the wet night and lights a lantern. The bed has been made up with an old patchwork quilt and a red blanket. I can see he has done his best to make the room cosy and I am just summoning up a 'thank you' when he says, 'And there's an extra blanket in the cupboard if you get cold.' He sounds cross that he has gone to such trouble for me. He turns back to the stairs. 'You'd best get the rest o' your things in before the rain worsens.'

Up and down the stairs I go, in and out of the rain. I heave the last suitcase along the landing. Once inside my room, I close the door firmly and sit down on the bed. I am shaking all over and breathing hard. I take off my boots and my wet coat and dress. I climb under the blankets and close my eyes, suddenly aware of how exhausted I am. The bed is so soft I feel that I am sinking into sleep itself. My breathing slows at last. The pillow has a faintly animal smell — summer hay and feathers and lambs' wool, so different from the clean starched linen of home.

'What am I doing here?' I whisper. 'How has this happened?'

Cousin Clarence, my brain replies. The hard *c* sounds are guttural, disgusted; his name has become a curse. *Cousin Clarence made this happen.*

But thick clouds of sleep are drifting across my thoughts now, eclipsing Cousin Clarence, the man called Thomas Walters, George the black pony, and the whole ghastly day.

6

I am woken by the smell of frying bacon. It takes me a moment to remember where on earth I am. Then the horrors of the past few days creep back into my mind one by one like a horde of shadows. I take a big breath, kneel up on the bed, open the curtains and look out of the little square window.

Oh! My window looks directly out on to the lake. Mist is rising from the still water in pale, ghostly breaths. The huge fells rise up from this swimming greyness – vast, ancient mountains, somehow bigger than they have ever been before. Despite growing up on the shores of Gosswater, I have never seen it like this. Our southern corner of the lake was tame by comparison – the neat little bay in which I was forbidden to swim (even on the hottest of summer days), its shore framed with marble pillars and trimmed topiary. This view of the lake is something quite different – something wild and magnificent: the same mountains, but here they are close and real – not just a backdrop for afternoon tea. I open the window and crane my neck, but I can't quite see Gosswater Hall from here: it is hidden behind an outcrop of grey rock and wind-twisted pine trees.

The cold air and the smell of bacon make me suddenly hungry, so I decide to venture downstairs. No one has brought me hot water, and no one has laid out my clothes for me. *This is how it is now, Agatha*, my brain says. *Stiff upper lip. You will be back at Gosswater Hall before you know it.*

So I wash quickly using the jug of ice-cold water on the wash stand, and I plait my hair. I unpack one of my better dresses and consider wearing it – just to show Thomas that although I have no choice but to stay here for the time being, I clearly don't *belong* here. Common sense prevails, though, and I put on some-thing warm and woollen instead. I make my way down the narrow staircase.

A cloud of cooking-smoke greets me as I make my way into the kitchen. Thomas has his back to me. 'Breakfast?' he says. He doesn't turn around.

'Yes. Please. Good morning.'

I sit down at the tiny table and look for a napkin to put upon my lap, but there isn't one.

'Tea?'

'Yes. Please.'

Thomas places my breakfast in front of me, along with a chipped mugful of steaming tea. It is rather dark and has been made with milk rather than lemon, but I decide not to say anything. Thomas doesn't smile – he doesn't even look at me – and in a way I am glad. He may well believe himself to be my father, but he must have realized that we are very different creatures from very different worlds, and that this is all a terrible mistake.

'Thank you,' I say politely. I've never before been served breakfast by someone who isn't a servant. 'Are you eating too?'

'I've had mine, don't you worry.' He turns back to the sideboard. 'It's a busy time o' year for me now, with Christmas around the corner, so you'll need to pull your weight. You can make the breakfast tomorrow. And you'll be cleanin' all that mud off the stairs too.'

It's the most he has said to me so far. His voice is growly and stilted – as if he's not used to speaking in full sentences. *Not to a human being, anyway*, I think, remembering his gentle chat with the pony.

Thomas bangs about at the sink – washing a plate, scrubbing a frying pan. I watch him. I don't know the first thing about how to cook breakfast, or how to clean up after it. And I've never scrubbed stairs in

my life. I think back to last night. Did I notice the
trail of mud my boots left on the stairs? I certainly
noticed it coming down this morning – all dried
into crusts. I've never *needed* to notice things like
that before. Suddenly I am feeling very sorry for
myself – my eyes start prickling and my throat
tightens. I pick up my knife and burst an enormous
egg yolk: it oozes hot and yellow all over the thin
strip of bacon and the single piece of dry toast. It
isn't much of a breakfast – no cinnamon crumpets
or spiced apple turnovers – but it still transports
me back to that dreadful meal with Clarence the
day before yesterday . . . *'You are illegitimate. You are
nobody . . .'*

Thomas is standing in the kitchen doorway. He is
saying something.

'What?'

He clears his throat. 'I said, I'll be outside.'

'Oh.'

'Don't you like your breakfast?'

I have hardly touched it. 'Yes – it's quite adequate.
Thank you . . .'

I nearly say, 'Thank you, *Thomas*,' but manage to
stop myself just in time. It would sound too much like
I was addressing an equal, or – worse – a footman. *How
ought I to address him? 'Mr Walters' doesn't feel quite right,
and I'm certainly not going to call him 'Father' . . .*

He goes outside and the back door closes behind

him. Then I hear that same sound I heard last night – a chattering and flapping; then a honking – like a badly blown hunting horn. *Ducks don't sound like that . . .*

I open the back door. There is a vegetable patch beneath the kitchen window, and then a steep, scruffy lawn that goes all the way down to the water's edge, where a rowing boat is moored. Actually, it is more of a meadow than a lawn – great tufts of grass grow wild and ragged, and much of it has gone to clover.

At the side of the house is a large shed with a stable door. The top half of the door is open, and I can just make out a tall shadow moving about inside – it's Thomas. *What is he doing?* I tiptoe closer.

Suddenly the bottom half of the door flies open and a torrent of white birds pour out, honking and jostling. They head straight towards me. I shriek and lift my skirts to move out of the way, but the stream parts like a white-feathered waterfall and they run either side of me, down the garden towards the lake.

Thomas appears behind the last of the birds, shepherding them out of the shed.

'Geese!' I say, breathless. I drop my skirts again, brush them down and try to look composed.

Thomas looks at me directly, and it is not the kindest of looks. 'Aye. Geese. Our family's kept geese here for generations. That's why it's called Gosswater – didn't you know? Goss is the old word for goose.'

'Oh.' I usually enjoy discovering facts like this, but the geese have spooked me, and there's something else too. He said *our* family. *Ours*. I don't want anything to do with a family of goose farmers – I'm an *Asquith*. Geese may feature in our family crest, but that's as close as I ever want to get to one.

'Good things to keep, geese,' Thomas says. 'Eggs, company, roast dinners, and they're as good as guard dogs.'

I think of the legend of the Queen Stone – the vicious geese attacking the rebels and saving the crown . . . At least these ones don't seem too fierce now. Some of them are grazing on the lower stretches of the grass, others are swimming on the mirror-green lake. But one goose has not gone down to the water's edge. It is smaller than the others, and the tip of its orange beak is black. It stands beside Thomas's leg, looking up at him like a devoted puppy.

'Mornin', Susan,' Thomas says, bending down to smooth the feathers on her plump white chest. For the first time since we met, his dark brow lifts and I can see the traces of a smile around his lips. 'I've had this one nearly fourteen years. Hasn't laid an egg since I can't remember when, but she's never goin' in the pot. Follows me about like a lamb. Followed me halfway to Penrith once, didn't you, Sue?'

There is something so natural about the way he uses the goose's name that it makes me aware of the awkward gaps in our sentences. Neither of us knows what to call the other, so there are ghostly little silences where our names should be.

'So you are a farmer, then – a *goose* farmer?' I say.

'Aye,' he says in a low voice. His eyes burn darkly, as if I have accused him of something. 'This farm, these geese. This is me. This is all there is, I'm afraid, Lady Agatha.'

Susan the goose waddles over and sniffs at my shoes with her bright beak, then she stretches out her neck and hisses at me.

I step back, suppressing a scream. A nasty little demon inside me wants to kick the stupid creature away. My foot twitches.

'Be nice,' Thomas growls.

Is he talking to me or the goose?

Thomas takes a handful of grain from his pocket and Susan nibbles it from his open palm. 'You'd better get used to them,' he says. 'You can look after them when I'm away at market. It'll save me payin' one of the village boys.'

Has he lost his mind?

'Me? Look after farm animals?'

But Thomas is walking away, scattering grain as he goes, and Susan follows. She clacks her black-tipped beak and sways down the meadow to join the others.

I watch, staying exactly where I am at the top of the grassy bank.

The geese honk and barge about Thomas's feet – a silly, noisy, feathered family. And I am not part of it: I am a stranger here.

Alone.

7

I don't see Thomas for the rest of the day. He says he has to take some geese to a butcher's shop in Penrith. They've put in an order for Christmas – just two days away now. I stand in the yard and watch him load the carcasses on to the pony cart. He holds them by their floppy necks, and my stomach turns.

Thomas climbs into his seat and flicks the reins. George turns neatly and sets off at a steady trot. Neither of them looks back.

Well, Agatha, my brain says. And I feel an unexpected thrill as I go back into the empty cottage and close the door behind me. *Time to have a proper look around.*

It doesn't take long. The cottage has only seven rooms in total and they are all small and sparsely furnished.

Yet it feels comfortable – the windows fit snugly in their frames, the floorboards don't creak and the bannister doesn't wobble. It might be an old and crooked cottage, but it is as tight as a little ship: everything is practical, purposeful, well-made.

I look inside all Thomas's cupboards, peer behind the kitchen dresser, check under his bed. I'm looking for something secret: hidden treasure or a stash of bank notes – something to make sense of Clarence's gleeful words: *Thomas Walters is nothing more than a common thief* . . . I feel a quick pinch of hypocrisy, thinking of the stolen King Stone. Like father, like daughter?

But my brain rejects the thought immediately: *He is not your father, Agatha. And you are not a thief* . . .

Then I find something at the back of a drawer – an old envelope. Money, perhaps? I look inside. No – just some dried rose petals, a goose feather and a lock of golden hair – sentimental mementoes. Perhaps Thomas isn't quite as tough as he seems.

I continue my search but the only other interesting thing I find – wrapped up in a dirty cloth at the back of a kitchen cupboard – is a bag of tools.

A thief would need tools, my brain says – *for forcing windows or jemmying doors* . . . I try to imagine Thomas wielding a crowbar, but I just can't make it fit. His cottage feels honest. Poor, but honest.

A great wave of rage rises from nowhere.

'It's all WRONG,' I say out loud, and I slam the

cupboard door shut with a resounding BANG.

How can Thomas be my father? Whether he is a common thief or just a poor goose farmer – how can he possibly be anything to do with me?

'I am Lady Agatha Asquith of Gosswater!' I say, meeting the steely gaze of my own eyes, reflected in the kitchen window. Father – or perhaps I should say, the Twenty-Ninth Earl of Gosswater – told me once that I have the stubborn chin of an Asquith. How can that be the case if I don't have Asquith blood in my veins? I look at my profile, reflected in the window. I straighten my spine, pull my shoulders back and lift my chin. Yes – it *is* stubborn. It's a strong, noble, Asquith chin. It's the sort of chin that doesn't give in easily. Cousin Clarence doesn't have a chin at all. Not a proper one. Then it occurs to me: what if Clarence is lying? After all, I never actually *saw* what was written in the will he was waving about at the breakfast table. What if he has persuaded Thomas to play along with his ruse so that he can get me out of his way? What if he has *paid* him? Yes – that must be it! Relief rinses all the rage and fear away. Thomas isn't my father at all – of course he isn't! All I need to do is prove that Cousin Clarence is lying and I can go home . . .

It is dark when Thomas returns. I have made a pot of tea and assembled some things to eat – bread, cheese and a slab of fruitcake. I cooked a Cumberland sausage

44

I found in the larder, and I think it looks quite appetizing now I have cut off the blackened bits. It has taken me hours and I feel oddly proud that I have managed to prepare this meal all by myself, even if it is more of a performance than a sincere gesture. I am determined to show Thomas that I am not a spoilt little miss.

'Good evening,' I say, when Thomas stoops in through the front door. Now that I feel sure we are not related and that I will be going back to Gosswater Hall soon, I feel more generous towards him.

He looks at the feast on the table, takes his cap and coat off and slowly unwinds his scarf.

'I was saving that sausage,' he says.

'I can wrap it up again if you like.'

'No. We might as well have it now it's . . . cooked.'

I pour the tea and glance towards the freshly cleaned stairs: I hope he notices my hard work. My poor fingers are raw from scrubbing them with freezing-cold water.

'How was the drive to Penrith?' I ask sweetly.

He shrugs as he sits down: 'Er . . . all right. Thick mist up at Ramskull Pass – as usual.' He eyes me cautiously – I have unsettled him.

I decide not to say anything at all for a while. We eat in silence. There is a noise from outside – something being knocked over – and Thomas goes to investigate.

'Fox,' he says when he comes in again. 'Fox gets bold this time o' year.'

He says 'Fox' as if it is the creature's Christian name; as if he and Fox are old friends – or old enemies. He sits down at the table.

It's the right moment, Agatha.

I pour more tea. 'Do you mind me asking, Thomas – I've been at Gosswater Hall all these years – just a few miles away – why wait until now to come forward as my father?'

He looks at me, then looks down at the table. It is a moment before he speaks. 'I came to see you at the Hall last year, but I was turned away. Then I got a message out o' the blue that the earl had died and I should come and get you. So I did.' He pushes his chair back and takes his plate to the sink. 'That's all there is to it.'

If he really was your father, he'd be happy to talk about it, surely? my brain hisses. *Keep going, Agatha . . .*

'I was thinking that Cousin Clarence might have . . .'

But Thomas interrupts me. 'He has nothin' to do with any of it.'

'Did he pay you?'

He turns. He looks me dead in the eye, and I am surprised at the readiness of the anger glaring back at me. '*What?*'

'Did Clarence pay you to take me in?'

I watch the fury rise into his chest. 'That's what you think of me, is it, then? A crook? The sort o' man to trade bairns like cattle?'

'No! I just thought . . .'

'That it must be about *money*? That everythin' can be bought and sold? Well, that's *Asquiths* all over, that is.'

I can't hold back any longer – anger rips its way out of me, hot and savage: 'How *dare* you insult my family like that? You take me from my home and bring me *here*? You expect me to put up with *this*?' I am suddenly disgusted by the miserable food on the table, furious that this stranger made me scrub his filthy stairs; my raw hands burn with rage.

Thomas stares at me, trembling now. 'I don't understand the first thing about you people,' he growls, and heads for the doorway.

'Thomas, wait!'

But he has gone.

I go straight to my room and close the door, shutting out the argument and the anger and that dreadful look on Thomas's face . . . I pinch the candle flame and sit there in the blackness, staring out of the window while my breathing slows. It is a clear night – cold and starlit. The huge, dark shoulders of the fells surround us, huddling us all together – the cottage, the valley, the sheep, bold Fox, and the moon-bright lake. I touch the window pane and my fingertips stick to the cold glass – there will be a frost tonight.

I am thinking about what Thomas said – that he tried to visit me at Gosswater Hall last year, but I can't bring myself to believe it. It doesn't make any sense.

And what did he mean when he said he didn't understand 'you people'? The Asquith family? The aristocracy? Anyone more privileged than a goose farmer? There was something terrible in his eyes when he hissed the word '*Asquiths*'.

Beneath the blanket, I curl up into a tight ball, my forehead touching my knees.

Nothing can hurt you, Agatha, if you don't let it in.

I have done this since I was tiny. All those times when Mother told me to go and play somewhere else, or when Father refused to see me for days on end.

I squeeze my eyes shut. I need to sleep. It is Christmas Eve tomorrow – and it is Father's funeral. My black silk dress had to remain at Gosswater Hall, and the only other black dress I have is a woollen one, rather worn. It will have to do. It is hanging up ready on the narrow rail in the corner, suspended in the darkness like a spectre. Miss McCarthy the housekeeper had put a little present in the trunk for me – a box containing a smart new black hat. There was a note: *For the earl's funeral. I will be thinking of you, dear Agatha. With love from Miss McCarthy.* I wonder if Clarence knows how fond of me Miss McCarthy was; I wonder if that was why he dismissed her.

All this is just a game to Clarence – the thrill of the hunt! He wants to destroy me – the scraggy little fox cub – so that he can ride out of the forest blooded and

48

triumphant. He has plotted and planned so that Goss-water Hall and all its treasures can be his.

My eyes flick open in the darkness.

Not all *the treasures of Gosswater Hall, Clarence* . . . I am thinking of the heavy bundle at the bottom of my travelling bag. I throw back the patchwork quilt and the knitted blanket. I burrow into my bag, rummaging through petticoats and nightdresses. At last my hands close around it. The King Stone is not Clarence's any more: it is mine – my connection with home, and the person I used to be. Back beneath the bed clothes, I unwrap the opal. Even in the dark, it glimmers with strange, electric colours.

I fall asleep holding the stone against my stomach, keeping it warm as if it were an egg waiting to hatch.

8

Although he considers me an illegitimate outcast, Cousin Clarence has allowed me to attend the earl's funeral. He has even sent one of the best carriages to collect me — the one with the family crest embossed on the glossy dark-blue doors.

It's not for your benefit, Agatha, my brain says, as I skirt the puddles in Thomas's yard and make my way towards the carriage. *Clarence would be so embarrassed if you arrived at Gosswater Hall in Thomas's cart . . .*

The carriage is waiting for me out on the lane. I go down the track towards it, taking care not to scuff my shoes on the sharp stones. I am determined not to look back at the cottage. I know Thomas is still there at the door, watching me go. He offered to come with me: 'A child shouldn't go to a funeral alone,' he murmured.

But I said, 'I'll be fine, thank you,' and swept straight past him. I do not want to be indebted to that man for any kindness. He has not apologized for the things he said last night, and neither have I. The argument is still there in the house, lingering, like the smell of the burnt Cumberland sausage.

There is a rustling from the bushes just in front of me and a creature darts out – wet, red-brown fur, white-tipped tail. *Fox.* He stops, turns and looks at me with bright, gold eyes, and then hares away up the track, over the lane and into the bushes. Out hunting? Or being hunted? The moment has left my heart beating a little faster.

Clarence's driver nods politely and helps me up into the carriage. I sink into the plush blue velvet, my lungs taking long, loving breaths of cherry wood and beeswax polish. It has only been a few days, but the luxuries of Gosswater Hall already feel as if they belong to a different lifetime. My brain mutters something about today being a farewell to Father, not a chance to mourn all the material things I have lost, but I ignore it. I feel horribly homesick and selfish. I don't want to grieve for Father. How could he have left me in this ghastly mess?

The journey goes quickly. I try to keep track of each turning and landmark so that I can find my way back to Gosswater Hall by myself, but one murky sheep field looks so much like the next that I eventually give up. As we turn through the high iron gates of home, we meet carriages that have brought guests from all over the county, and we form a stately procession, following the private road across the estate towards the lake.

The house itself is just on the other side of those fir trees – so close it feels cruel. I'll be able to see it properly in a moment. Both of my hands are pressed flat against the carriage windows, and the tip of my nose too. My breath fogs the glass. At last it emerges – the huge dark shape of it, the cold symmetry of its towers and turrets – and I feel a pang of disappointment: it is quite unchanged, as if it hasn't noticed that I have gone. Does it care that Clarence is its master now? Or that Father is dead?

The hearse carrying the late earl's coffin is at the front of the procession, pulled by a pair of giant black horses with plumes attached to their bridles. It reminds me of Mother's funeral – just a few years before. It could almost be the same occasion. Mother died in winter too. Her heart gave out on a day just like this one – all frost and stillness and bare-bone branches. I watch the ice-gilded estate as it wheels past my window, and I smooth the skirts of my worn woollen dress. I think about the dresses I have left behind – the green velvet, with its fitted bodice and shimmering liquid skirts; the black silk – so soft and cool it is like touching midnight. Mother always said there was comfort to be found in such loveliness. I try to picture her face – powdered, pale and delicate, her skin as soft as cobwebs. Mother smiled more often than Father did, but her smiles were faded and distant – as if she were in love with her daydreams of the past. I can only remember her getting truly angry once . . . I tried to escape from my room one night so that I could go to see an outdoor performance of *Romeo and Juliet* at Windermere; 'I always knew you would turn out wild and wayward,' she'd screamed, and then went to lie down in her room for several days. Mother insisted on keeping me safe, like a bird in a cage. They stopped taking me anywhere some years ago – even to church – and visitors stopped coming to Gosswater Hall too. They didn't explain why. Neither of them ever talked to me about anything important.

The carriages park in a row on the shingled bank of the lake. The horses stamp and nod gravely to one another, like gentlemen commencing a duel. The doors of the carriages are opened and the black-clad mourners pour out like insects. They form a busy-looking line and I wait for them all to shuffle past before I join them, unwilling to suffer the humiliation of anyone actually speaking to me. Many of them will know who I am – after all, I am the only child here – but will they know that I am no longer Lady Agatha and that I am living in a goose farmer's cottage? And how on earth will I introduce myself to those who *don't* know me? I can hardly bear the shame and confusion of it all.

Today, for once, I just want to be invisible.

The boats are here, waiting to take us out to Skelter Island — the cemetery island in the middle of the lake. We move down the jetty in silence and, one by one, we are helped into the boats by black-gloved servants. I don't recognize anyone apart from Cousin Clarence, and he does not choose to look at me. He is talking to an elderly lady wearing a large-brimmed black hat and a necklace heavy with emeralds. They walk carefully along the jetty, arm in arm. The lady seems to be very frail. I notice that Clarence is wearing one of Father's most expensive cravats — the orange one with the pheasants. I don't think it is *at all* the sort of thing one should wear to a funeral.

I look down at the frosty slats of the jetty. The dark wood is etched with patterns of ice — silvery veins and frost-thorns. My black-patent footsteps turn them to grey mush. My breath is a shiver of steam in the cold morning air.

The first boats are already leaving, the oars pushing through the cold, still water with even little splashes. When, eventually, I am the only one left standing there on the jetty, something horrible happens.

I don't know why, but instead of looking down at the boat I am about to climb aboard, I glance at the boat that has just cast off, and I find that the elderly lady who was talking to Cousin Clarence is looking back at me. Her eyes are staring, huge and fixed, and her mouth opens in an *O* of terror. I stare back at her, frozen. The elderly lady's hand goes up to her throat as if she is suffocating, and then she collapses into the bottom of the boat. A blonde woman sitting next to her screams in fright, and the sound pierces the cold air, ringing around the high, rocky banks of the lake until it feels as if the fells themselves are screeching. A gulp of cormorants takes to the sky in a black, splashing panic. Suddenly people are shouting and fussing, and the boat rocks dangerously as people stand to look and move to help.

'Is she dead?' the blonde woman asks. 'Is she dead?'

Someone has lifted the elderly lady out of the boat and placed her on the jetty, just a few feet away from where I am standing. Her body is limp and her face is grey.

Yes. She is dead.

9

After the elderly lady's body has been carried back to the coaches, the boats resume their journey towards the island. I wonder who she was and how she knew Father. I can still see her face – spellbound, petrified. My shoulders rise and fall quickly and I feel sick. I hold on to the side of the boat, gripping it through my black kid gloves. I feel quite unreal. The misty world around us is eerily quiet. It is as if the boat has drifted into the underworld: I am surrounded by the dead. I am one of them.

The oars splash and the boat pushes through the still water.

Someone speaks. 'Poor Millicent.'

I turn towards the stern. It is the blonde lady who screamed. She still looks shaken – her hands clutched together in a knot. Her blonde hair is wound into shining, golden coils, all pinned up under a stylish hat of black feathers which tremble when she speaks. Sitting very close beside her is Cousin Clarence, patting her arm in what he presumably thinks is a reassuring manner. In all the confusion of people getting in and out and in again, I have somehow ended up in Clarence's boat.

'Yes, indeed, poor Millicent,' Clarence echoes, though it doesn't sound terribly heartfelt. He straightens his cravat.

I've heard the name Millicent before. She was a great-aunt on Mother's side, though I never actually met her. We very rarely had visitors at Gosswater Hall. So *that* was Great-aunt Millicent . . .

'She travelled a long way to be at your uncle's funeral today, Clarence,' the elegant blonde lady goes on. 'It must simply have been too much for her.'

Clarence pats the lady's arm again and nods sympathetically. 'She was very close to the earl, I believe – a dear friend.'

I almost laugh. Father didn't give two hoots about Great-aunt Millicent.

'Oh, Clarence, it really is such a delight to meet you at last.' The lady unknots her hands and takes his warmly. She seems to have recovered from the shock remarkably quickly. 'Whereabouts is your own estate? Berkshire?'

Clarence smiles and nods: 'Four hundred acres.'

The lady smiles too and tilts her chin. 'We haven't seen nearly enough of you Asquiths over recent years. Understandable, of course, that poor Henry and Catherine would want to take a step back after that dreadful business . . . The curse of the Queen Stone, people called it.' She sighs. 'A tragedy that such a gem should be lost.'

The curse of the Queen Stone? I've never heard of that before. Perhaps it explains everything that is happening. Perhaps *I* am cursed . . .

'Mmmm.' Clarence nods, as if he is agreeing. He smiles slowly. 'I do like your earrings, Baroness. Three carats?'

She touches the diamond in her right ear, blushes and says, 'Four. And please do call me Odelia.'

Clarence grins and shuffles a bit closer.

'Do tell me all about your magnificent King Stone, dear Clarence,' she continues. 'I've heard it's one of the largest black opals in the world.'

They talk about jewels for some time – it seems the baroness knows a great deal about them. Eventually the conversation comes back to Great-aunt Millicent – via the value of her emerald necklace . . .

'The more I think about it, the more I am sure it must have been a fit of some kind,' the baroness is saying. 'Poor Millicent. An apoplexy or something. What a terrible way to go.'

Was it a fit? I wonder. *She was looking at me when she collapsed − looking right into my eyes . . .* I try not to picture Great-aunt Millicent's face again, but I can't help it. Every time the hideous image opens its mouth, my insides cramp with fright. *What was it she saw?* I try to imagine myself from her perspective. A girl at her father's funeral, all in black. A small figure, standing on the icy jetty by herself, the mist rising around her from the still water. A sad image, perhaps, but not a petrifying one, surely? No. It can't have been me. The baroness is right − it must have been a fit. Apoplexy.

I look ahead to Skelter Island as it emerges from the mist − a grey hulk, strewn with leafless trees and studded with tombstones. Beyond the trees I can see the gloomy shadow of the church. The bell tolls, slowly, the low note dulled by the moisture in the heavy air. A coot calls as if in reply, its shrill bleat startling in the stillness.

We have stopped moving now. The boat behind us gently bumps into our stern and the baroness grips Clarence's elbow. He smiles at her − a broad, toothy, 'eligible' smile . . . Another wave of nausea washes over me. The boats rock to and fro, waiting their turn to moor up.

This is how Asquith funerals have been for centuries. The first Asquiths to be buried on Skelter Island were victims of the Black Death. It was thought safer to put them here − to avoid the disease spreading into the earth from the rotting bodies. Then island burials became a family tradition. This is where Asquiths go when we die. The church that stands today was built in the mid-1600s and over the years vaults and tombs and statues were added too. It is a weird place – beautiful in its way, but eerie. Living people are intruders on this island of the dead.

A red-haired boy is helping to tie up the boats, catching the ropes and tying swift knots. He takes my hand when I climb out and gives me friendly grin. He must be about my age, I think – or at least he is about my height, which amounts to the same sort of thing. I wonder if he works for the undertakers.

The coffin is lifted on to the shoulders of the pall-bearers, and we all follow it through the leafless trees, past the crumbling gravestones and vaults. Clarence and the baroness are just in front of me. She takes his arm, and he swaggers like a jackdaw.

'And how has the child taken it all?' the baroness says, glancing back at me sympathetically. 'The passing of the earl, and so on?'

'Oh, she's fine,' Clarence murmurs, allowing himself another lustful look at the baroness's diamond earrings. His eyes meet mine and he makes a shooing gesture, as if I were an annoying fly.

I glower at him, dropping back a step or two, but I can still just hear their conversation. 'She's living with her real family now,' the baroness says. 'Is that right?'

Clarence nods, his lips pouted in a performance of sadness.

'Well – I think that's probably for the best. I know Henry and Catherine must have been fond of her, but blood is blood. When all's said and done, one needs to be with one's own kind.'

'My thoughts exactly, Odelia. I shall miss little Agatha terribly, but it really is for the best.'

My breath has caught in my chest. She knows that the earl and countess were not my real parents. I stumble over a tree root but, somehow, I keep walking. My feet automatically follow the procession of polished black boots.

They are all talking about me now, and it is as if I really am invisible: 'One can never be too careful when one doesn't know about a creature's breeding,' says a large gentleman in a fur coat, joining the conversation, and his wife nods sagely. 'I got a cross-bred pup once, though I paid for a pedigree – the wretched thing was a nightmare. I had to send it back. It's the same thing really.'

'Bad blood will out,' Clarence agrees loudly. 'One can only suppose they took her in out of pity originally. Like a stray cat.'

Hatred and humiliation billow within me like thunder clouds.

'Oh, what a dreadful day!' the baroness sighs, her

hat-feathers quivering with emotion. 'First Henry, and now Millicent. I feel shocked to my very core.'

And I feel shocked to my very core too, *Baroness*.

It seems my illegitimacy is common knowledge; everyone here at the funeral knows the earl and countess were not my real parents. I feel an odd sense of weightlessness as I am forced to accept this truth. Who am I without my parents? I am untethered, drifting – like a windborne balloon. And yet, of all the unbelievable things Clarence told me over that miserable breakfast, this one is perhaps the most bearable. A small part of me was almost hoping it was true . . .

It wasn't that you were impossible to love, Agatha – it was that you were never really theirs.

The procession has stopped at the latest Asquith family vault – a monstrosity of marble slabs and columns. Mother's coffin is in there somewhere, but Father requested to be buried in the earth instead. He said he had no intention of spending eternity lodged on a shelf like a forgotten pickle jar.

Next to the vault, there is a wet, rectangular pit in the ground. The mourners edge around it, forming a thin, black crescent, and we all watch as the Twenty-Ninth Earl of Gosswater is slowly lowered in. It looks cold in there. Cold and wet. I shudder.

Grief is a complicated feeling, I think. I wonder if it is more straightforward if it follows the footprint of love, rather than trailing in the wake of cold indifference.

He wasn't much of a father. If he loved me at all, he loved me at arm's length. I remember an afternoon when I was reading alone in the library and Father came in with his book – I don't know why I remember this so vividly. He saw me, stopped, turned, and went to find somewhere else to read. I must have been about seven years old. Such a tiny moment of rejection, but one that took root in my heart. Suddenly I feel dreadfully lonely and lost. Thomas was right – a child shouldn't go to a funeral alone. My throat burns with sadness – grief for the only parents I have ever known, all mixed up with a lifetime of loneliness and anger . . .

But then Cousin Clarence turns around and looks at me, and I swallow the tears back down.

Why are you crying, Agatha? his eyes say. *The Earl of Gosswater was nothing to you. You have no right to grieve for him. You're not an Asquith, remember? You're nobody . . .*

Sobs bang inside my ribs like swallowed coughs. I glare at Clarence as he turns his back on me once more. Perhaps if I glare hard enough, his black overcoat will burst into flames . . .

Then I realize I am being watched. An old man is standing by the tombs, leaning on a spade. The dirt on his clothes is the same colour as the mud in the rectangular pit. He must be the gravedigger. He is very bony – his hands are more knuckle than flesh. He makes me think of the gravediggers in *Hamlet*, but they are clowns, riddling as they dig, joking with the bones, and this man is not a clown. There is something very odd about him . . . His lips seem to be moving as he looks at me. His gnarled fingers tap the handle of the spade, and one of his thin legs jigs up and down, as if it wants to be dancing. Then he gives me a hideous toothless grin.

I can't bear it – any of it.

I turn quickly and walk away, walking faster and faster until I find I am running. Away from the gravedigger and the wet pit and the coffin, away from the callous glances of Cousin Clarence, and the strangers who hardly knew my father but seem to know all about me.

I run until all these horrors are far behind me, somewhere in the winter mist, and it is just me, the trees, and the forgotten tombs.

IO

I reach out to touch the trunks of tall silver birches either side of me; I listen to a robin singing in the branches above; I kick through the mulch of leaves and breathe in the clean, damp, earthy smell. I feel as if I have escaped.

Here is an unusual tomb. I stop and look at it. It is not as grand as all the others on the island. It is smaller and simpler. The stone is such a pale grey it is almost silver. Ivy and dog roses are growing over it, framing the wooden door, clinging devotedly to the shimmering stone. The inscription is just one word:

BELOVED

That's all – no name, and no dates. I look all around for some other clue as to whose tomb this might be but

I can't see a plaque anywhere. The tomb is close to the edge of the island and behind it the trees and bushes have been cleared away so that there is a clear view out to the lake. As I peer through the rising mist, I can just make out the faint silhouette of Gosswater Hall on the far bank. Then I notice something else – in the bark of the silver birch growing beside the tomb, someone has carved the shape of a rose. The tree has healed the cut into a dark, curving scar.

A rose . . . It makes me think of the words Father spoke before he died – something about a rose and eternity. I have no idea what he meant, but it was his last peaceful moment before those final wracking gasps. *Poor Father.* Sobs convulse in my chest again and this time I let them go. The grief floods out – grateful, released. Tears warm my cheeks and throat. I allow myself to think of Father at the end, and in all the years before. I say goodbye to him, and then I say goodbye to the gruff old man who was not my father after all. After a while, the tears come more gently. I reach into the pocket of my coat to find a handkerchief, but my hand finds something else too – my little mother-of-pearl hand mirror. I open it and look myself right in my haunted, reddened eyes.

There is someone else I must say goodbye to, and this is the right place for such a parting. I do not know yet who I really am, but I now know who I am *not*.

I take a long, slow breath, and I imagine the soul of

Lady Agatha Asquith stepping out of my body. It is like running a wet paintbrush through watercolour. A smooth, sliding movement and then she is there, waiting beside me like a shadow.

Goodbye, Lady Agatha.

The shadow walks towards the tomb, pauses and then steps through the silver stone.

She is gone. I feel exactly the same. I feel different. The robin sings again.

Who am I now?

Just Aggie, my brain says. *Just plain Aggie.*

For some reason, I feel the urge to take my gloves off and look at my pink hands: stripping something away – looking for something beneath. I press my warm palms to my face, my fingers covering my eyes.

There is a sound. Leaves crunching behind me. The robin stops singing.

My hands drop to my sides. I turn around and see the gravedigger coming towards me through the trees. He limps and jigs along, dead branches gathering and cracking beneath the spade that drags behind him.

My heart thumps. I feel horribly alone.

'What do you want?' I say. Somehow my voice sounds confident, authoritative – the legacy of dear departed Lady Agatha. What I really want to say is, *Don't come any closer.* I take a step back towards the tomb and place my hand on the smooth stone. It makes me feel safer.

'Yer one of 'em, aren't yer?' he says. The words are mangled by his toothless gums. 'An Asssquith. I seen the darkness in yer – starin' an' glarin' at his Lordship like yer'd kill him stone dead if yer could. That there's an Asquith child, says I.'

'I'm not an Asquith,' I manage to say. 'I'm nothing to do with them.'

He lunges closer to me, peering at my face. His eyes are bright red, bloodshot. 'An Assssquith o' Gossssswa-ter,' he says, spitting as he hisses. 'Y' know what Goss means, don't yer, little lady?'

'I do, as it happens.' And I stand a little taller. 'Goss means goose. Geese have been farmed on the banks of this lake for generations.'

The gravedigger laughs, and it is a disgusting sound – hard and hacking. 'Hah! Goose, little lady? *Goose?* . . .' He shuffles closer still. My back is pressed firmly against the tomb now. The gravedigger smells of alcohol, dirt, sweat. 'Goss is *ghost*. It's Gosswater for all the ghosts that haunt this island. Asquiths've never been ones for restin' peacefully. Too many dark secrets. Too much *unfinished business*.' He taps his bony red nose, as if I am supposed to know what that means. 'Might drive some folks mad, livin' here on an island wi' ghosts an' ghosts an' ghosts, but not me. An' there's a new one comin' soon – risin' up to right the wrongs of its sinful life. I can feel it.' He sniffs the air.

The church clock chimes the hour, and the gravedigger tilts his head. Then he whispers, 'Just seven days t' go. Seven days o' this month, seven days o' this year, seven days o' this century. Things creep through a crack like that – the crack between night an' day, between one year and t' next, between centuries. *Nasty* things seep an' creep through . . .'

I want to shove him away from me but there is something hypnotic about those wild, bloodshot eyes, the intense gaze, the bony hands that twitch and dance as he speaks . . .

'Mark my words, little lady – when that clock strikes midnight at the end o' this year, *somethin' will creep through the crack in time . . .*'

Someone is coming towards us – a quick, bouncing step. It is the red-haired boy who helped to tie up the boats. Thank goodness. 'They're ready for you to fill in the grave, Grandfather,' he says. 'The new earl wants t' see the headstone in place before he leaves.'

The gravedigger wipes his nose with the back of his hand and turns towards the boy. 'If he's in a hurry, then yer'd better help, hadn't yer? Gan an' get another spade, yer lazy brat.'

The boy cheerfully waves a spade in the air in reply. 'I'll be right behind you,' he says. 'I'll just help this young lady back to her boat first.'

The gravedigger grunts and limps away through the trees, muttering. I think he is still talking about ghosts.

'This way, miss,' the boy says, and I follow him, my head still spinning with the gravedigger's ominous words.

'Thank you,' I murmur.

'Bryn,' the boy says after a moment, putting his hand out to me as we walk. 'Bryn Black.'

I pause. I'm not used to people of this sort introducing themselves to me. I've certainly never shaken hands with anyone carrying a spade before. *Yes, but you're not Lady Agatha any more, are you?* my brain says.

I shake his hand. 'Aggie,' I say.

He smiles. He has a dimple in one cheek and freckles across his nose. His hair is short, red and wiry, like fox fur. 'That were Sexton Black. He lives here on the island and looks after the church and the graves. I live here too.' He looks towards the boats as he says this, as if he is currently plotting his escape.

'Did you hear what he said, your grandfather?' I ask.

'Let me guess: things creepin' through the gap between centuries? The wicked souls of Asquiths damned to roam restlessly about this island for ever and ever?'

I can't help smiling a little. He makes it sound so ridiculous.

'He didn't scare you, did he?'

'No, of course not,' I lie, pulling my kid gloves back on.

'Don't take any notice,' Bryn says. 'You can't think about stuff like that when you live somewhere like this. You'd go mad. Like him. It's just old bones here. Old bones . . . and new life.' He pauses and points at a tangle of tree roots that have forced a crumbling old gravestone up from the ground. 'These are the only things creepin' through cracks around here.'

I nod, and my brain believes him completely, but the superstitious part of me is still vibrating with fright.

'If a ghost really does appear on the stroke o' midnight, I'll eat my hat.'

I look at his mess of red hair. 'You're not wearing a hat, Bryn Black.'

'Ah,' he says. 'I'll have to eat yours, then.'

He has made me smile.

Is this how friends talk? I wonder, as Bryn helps me into the boat. I've never had a friend before.

Bryn is still talking: 'And a very nice hat it is too, Aggie. Can't be all bad, workin' at a big place like Gosswater Hall. They must pay you pretty well if you can afford nice things like that.'

I stare at him.

He thinks I am one of Clarence's servants. That's why he is so chatty with me, so easy and friendly. He saw a girl in a worn woollen skirt, standing at the back, hands clasped together, and he didn't see a lonely little

71

outcast — he saw a well-behaved servant.

A servant! But he is waving goodbye, turning around and walking back towards the tombs. A veil of mist rises up between us. It is too late to correct him now.

II

At Gosswater Hall, we always had a Christmas tree in the atrium. When I was small, we would often get up very early and travel to Penrith for the formal Christmas service, so Father could shake hands with important people and wish them a Merry Christmas. We would always be home in time for dinner, though – five courses – and then we would open our presents in the music room. My present was always a book I had asked for, though I knew Miss McCarthy was the one who had actually bought and wrapped it for me. Then, instead of going to our usual distant corners of the house to read, or do needle-work, we would all sit quietly together. When Mother was alive, she would sing carols at the piano in her trembling soprano voice: *Brightly shone the moon that night, though the frost was cruu-el . . .* There were no parlour games, no riddles or laughter, but there was at least a nod towards the occasion.

There is no Christmas at all at Thomas's house. It is a cold day, with shards of icy sunlight piercing holes through the thick cloud. 'Merry Christmas,' I say when I come down for breakfast. I feel I owe Thomas some sort of apology for yesterday morning when he offered to accompany me to the funeral and I refused. Heaven knows, it would have been ghastly for him to suffer the condescending comments of Clarence and his cronies; it was a kind thought.

He nods at my festive greeting. 'It's a day like any other.' He shrugs, and saws a slice of bread from the hard loaf on the kitchen table. 'There'll be no grand banquets here. There's always work to be done on a farm.'

Yes. There is always work to be done. My list of chores for the morning seems even longer than usual. Sweeping out the fireplace and bringing in a basket of logs is easy enough, but I hate collecting the eggs from the goose shed. I stay as far away from Susan as possible, edging around the piles of stinking straw whilst looking her dead in the eye. I won't let her see my fear. Then I have to groom George the pony. I have seen stable hands do this before – but, as Lady Agatha, I never did it myself. *Perhaps Aggie will be good at this sort of thing*, my brain says. I approach George gingerly, convinced he is about to bite my shoulder or kick me in the back, but he doesn't. I brush the dust from his black coat until it gleams. I get all the tangles out of his mane and tail. He lifts each hoof obediently so I can clean off the dried mud. When I am finished, George harrumphs gently and nuzzles his soft nose into the crook of my arm. I am suddenly very fond of him indeed. I put my arm around his neck, pressing my cheek against his warm, clean coat. 'Merry Christmas, George,' I murmur.

In the afternoon, I sit by the fire in the parlour reading *A Christmas Carol*. I try to pretend that this is just an ordinary day – that it doesn't matter. But when I read the description of the Cratchit family enjoying their meagre feast together, I have to put the book down and think about something else.

Thomas spends the whole afternoon outside, repairing the roof of the goose shed. I go to bed early, while he is still working. I am angry with him. It isn't just that there were no presents to open, no carols. If Thomas doesn't want to be my father, to be my *family*, why was he so keen to take me in? Am I his daughter or not? What is my name if I am no longer Agatha Asquith? Is this my life now – knowing nothing about myself, being nobody?

It takes me ages to fall asleep, and by the time I do, the goose-down pillow is damp with tears.

*

The next morning, I stand at the window watching Thomas getting the pony and cart ready. He strokes George's neck, talking to him as he tightens a buckle on the harness. I am struck by the contrast – how kind he is to the animals; how cold he is with me. When he looks up and sees me there, his brow darkens.

'I'll be gone awhile,' he calls, climbing up into the cart. 'Jobs to do in the village.'

My fists clench. I spent yesterday alone and went to bed angry. Today is going to be different.

'Wait!' I shout. 'I'm coming too.' I grab my coat and hat from the hallway and run out into the yard, the front door slamming behind me.

Thomas stares at me as I jump up on to the cart beside him. Then he tightens his lips and flicks the reins. George sets off at a comfortable trot.

We have reached the end of the track and are about to turn out on to the lane to the village when I hear a strange noise behind us – a clattering and flapping, like a flag in the wind. Thomas and I both turn around.

'Susan!'

Thomas stops the cart and leaps down.

The goose runs towards him down the track, her webbed feet flapping like paddles, her wings open.

'Susan – how in 'eck did you get out?' Thomas kneels down and she rushes to him. 'You're not to follow me – I've told you before!' She nibbles at his hair with her black-tipped beak. 'C'mon Sue. Let's get you back in the shed.'

Thomas stands up and walks back towards the cottage with the goose waddling happily along beside him.

He is back within a few minutes: 'Daft goose,' he says as he climbs up beside me.

'Daft goose,' I agree.

I think we are both smiling a little.

The cart starts to bump along once more and George's hooves clop rhythmically down the lane. Thomas and I have barely spoken since our argument the other night, when I managed to insult both him and his home, and he said he didn't understand the first thing about people like me. But, somehow, Susan has brought us to a truce.

'I'm sorry,' Thomas says, after a minute or two.

'About what?'

'About everythin'. About yesterday. I haven't had a proper Christmas in years. I think I've forgotten how. I should've thought more about it. About you.'

I nod. I am surprised at how quickly the anger has dissolved. 'And I'm sorry about those horrid things I said the other night. I didn't mean them. What you said about the Asquiths made me angry, that's all.'

'Aye. I shouldn't have said that.'

Are the Asquiths greedy? Obsessed with money? Clarence certainly is. I picture him on my rocking horse, gloating about being the richest, most eligible bachelor in the whole of England.

Then, as if he can read my mind, Thomas says, 'Don't tell me the new earl isn't a nasty piece o' work, though.'

'Funnily enough, I was just thinking that.'

The corners of Thomas's mouth twitch and his eyelids crinkle. For the first time, I feel there might be a spark of friendship between us.

'Where are we going?' I ask.

'The King's Head first, and then on to the village.'

'Why the King's Head?'

'Innkeeper's bought a goose for the Boxing Day lunch. And there's somethin' else I need to drop off too.' He nods at a square box by his feet. There appear to be some parcels of food in it and a fat envelope sealed with the Gosswater stamp.'

'Is that from Gosswater Hall?'

'Aye,' Thomas says. The trace of a smile has disappeared. 'Woah, there, George.'

We have arrived at the King's Head. It is very busy – there are people milling around outside in bright red coats, laughing loudly; steaming tankards clank together, a score of hounds whine and scrabble with excitement, a dozen gleaming horses stamp in the cold.

'The Boxing Day hunt,' I say. And my stomach goes cold. *Clarence will be here.*

12

'Why, there she is!' My cousin's voice, brassy as a bugle, cuts through the noise of the throng. 'Agatha, darling – we were just talking about you!'

Before I know what's happening, Clarence has yanked me down from the cart and wrapped his arms around me in a bear-like embrace. I would shriek if he hadn't squeezed all the breath from my body.

'This is Mr Charles Hetherington,' Clarence says, setting me down at last and introducing me to a small man with a narrow, mousey face. He is dressed in hunting gear, just like Clarence. 'Mr Hetherington was just enquiring after you, Agatha,' Clarence goes on. 'And I told him you were *very well*.'

Now I recognize him: Mr Hetherington is the

Asquith family solicitor. I've seen him once or twice before, scurrying up the corridor to Father's study, his case bursting with papers. He visited Gosswater Hall just a week ago, after Father took to his bed. Clarence thrusts me towards him. 'You *are* very well, aren't you, Agatha?'

'Quite well, thank you,' I say automatically, shaking Mr Hetherington's proffered hand. Clarence's white glove is gripping my shoulder tightly.

'You see?' Clarence says. 'She's perfectly well, Charles, perfectly happy. Nothing to worry about . . .'

Then I see Thomas looking at me from the pony-cart. His mouth has tightened and his brow is dark, as if he is furious with me, as if I have betrayed him some-how. *You just said you didn't like Clarence*, his eyes say. *I don't understand you. I don't understand the first thing about you people.* He can't hear the conversation – he doesn't know that I'm just a pawn in whatever game Clarence is currently playing. I want to explain; I try to wriggle from Clarence's grip and make my way back towards Thomas, but Brutus is at my cousin's heel – his slobbering, snarling mouth is level with my elbow.

Then Thomas calls out above the hubbub: 'I've come to return this, *your Lordship*.'

And there is a hush in the courtyard.

'*This?*' Clarence says jauntily, swinging around and giving Thomas a nonchalant smile. 'That's no way to talk about your *daughter*, is it, Walters?' Someone

80

behind me sniggers at the feeble joke.

'THIS,' Thomas growls. He picks up the square box and throws it down into the yard at Clarence's feet. A parcel of meat tumbles out and Brutus instantly tears into it. 'I don't want Asquith money, and I don't want the *scraps* from your table.'

'Now, now, my good man,' Clarence warns, stepping towards him. I take my chance and move quickly back to my side of the cart – out of my cousin's reach. 'There's no need to be like that, Walters. It's just a traditional St Stephen's Day box. I had my estate manager send it to you by way of thanks for . . . all your cooperation.'

'I don't want your thanks. I don't want anythin' from you Asquiths.'

'Well, I think you've made that quite clear,' Clarence sniffs. 'Perhaps you'd best be off now.' He turns his back on Thomas. 'A proud man,' I hear him sneer to Mr Hetherington. 'But Agatha is *very* happy living with him, I assure you.'

'That may be, your Lordship,' the solicitor squeaks, 'but I really do have to press you about those charitable commitments – they are legally stipulated—'

'All is as it should be, Mr Hetherington,' Clarence interrupts pleasantly. 'All is as it should be!' And he steers the solicitor away. 'What I *do* need you to do for me is find out about Moll Speedwell and her stash. Why has she got it and can we get it back? Will it come to me when the old bird falls off her perch?' They disappear into the crowd of red coats.

Thomas's face is still flushed and fuming. I reach out for him to help me up into the cart, but instead of taking my hand he passes me a goose carcass by its neck.

'Oh!'

'I'll collect you on my way back from the village,' he says in a low voice. 'Take the goose to the innkeeper, please, Agatha. He'll pay you.' And before I have a chance to say anything, George is trotting smartly away down the lane.

The goose swings lifelessly from my hand, its feathers unnervingly soft. Then Brutus and the fox hounds spot it. They surge around me, slavering. I hold the goose up above my head to stop it from being torn to pieces. My arms are shaking. *What if the dogs tear* me *to pieces instead?*

Clarence barks out a command, telling the master of hounds to bring the dogs to order, and at last they fall away to be readied for the hunt, lured by the promise of pursuit.

I tuck the floppy goose under my arm and take it around the back of the inn to the kitchen, where a man called Mr Tunn gives me a handful of coins. My head is still spinning and anger is fizzing in my chest, but I don't know who I am most angry at – Clarence or Thomas? I sit on a bench in the frosty morning light and wait for my thoughts to settle. Will Thomas come back for me? I wonder. He thinks I am two-faced. Is he right? I am aware of feeling torn down the middle – one hand is clinging to the familiarity of the past while the other is reaching out towards some kind of future. A future as Aggie.

'Goodbye!' Clarence calls, waving at me and smiling smugly. I don't wave back.

He thinks he has won, Aggie, my brain murmurs. *But he hasn't. You may not be Lady Agatha Asquith any more, but you still have his precious King Stone.* The thought is very heartening.

The hunt is assembled now. The blonde baroness from the funeral is there beside Clarence, mounted on a sturdy chestnut hunter. The party clatters away – a cacophony of blaring hunting horns and yelping hounds. *Poor Fox*, I think. I hope they don't get the one who lives near Thomas's cottage. It is a curious thing, the hunter becoming the hunted . . .

'Penny for your thoughts?' says a familiar voice.

I squint into the sunlight and see the red-haired boy from Skelter Island.

'Bryn!'

His face dimples, and he sits down beside me. 'Not that I've got a penny t' give you, Aggie.'

'Oh – I was just thinking about the hunt. Did you see them – out in all their finery?'

'Aye – quite a sight. I love the hounds and the

horses,' he says. Then: 'Do you think they could do with someone like me to help look after the dogs? Or the horses – I could be a stable boy or summat? Could you put in a good word for me at the Hall?'

I hesitate. Is this the moment to tell him that I'm not one of Clarence's servants?

I take one look at Bryn's open face, his freckled smile . . . 'I'm not really important enough for the earl to listen to me, Bryn.'

'Fair enough,' he says. 'I'd like to do that one day, though. Anythin' outdoors, away from that awful island. I'm good wi' animals. They're much nicer than people.'

I think about Brutus and the foxhounds, all barking and slavering.

Bryn smiles again. 'Not all people, of course. *Some* people are nice.' And he winks.

I laugh, and it feels like sunshine. I can't remember the last time I laughed. 'What are you doing here, Bryn?'

'Oh, I come t' the village once a week for supplies – and that usually means comin' here t' the inn too.' He makes a drinking gesture. 'Grandfather enjoys a drop or two.'

'Is he still talking about ghosts appearing on New Year's Eve?'

Bryn chuckles. 'Aye. It's an old tale, he says – at the stroke o' midnight, at the turn of the year, a restless soul will creep through the crack in time.'

'But why?'

He mimics the sexton's voice: 'T' right the wrongs o' the past!'

I know he is only joking, but the words send a tremor through my body. *If only it were true*, my brain whispers, *that a spirit from the past could somehow put everything right, and lift the curse of the Queen Stone . . .*

'Are you frit?'

'Frit?'

'Did I frighten you, talkin' about ghosts?'

'No, of course not, Bryn.'

'Prove it.' His eyes glitter.

'What do you mean?'

'Come out to Skelter Island on New Year's Eve. We'll go ghost-huntin'!'

'No Bryn, I don't think . . .'

He looks me in the eye and grins. 'I *dare* you, Aggie.'

Is Aggie the sort of girl to accept a dare? The sort of girl who would go ghost-hunting with her friend? Bryn seems to think so . . .

I meet his grin. 'New Year's Eve,' I say, and we shake hands.

Thomas collects me from the inn an hour or so later, just when I was about to give up hope and start walking. It is as if that spark of friendship never happened; I can't even picture that gently crinkled smile now the

85

dark frown is back in place again. I wish we'd never bumped into Clarence. I want to get back to where we were this morning, but I don't know how. I sigh and wrap a blanket around myself to keep the cold out. When the cart bumps over a rut in the road, something jingles in my coat pocket.

The money the innkeeper gave me for the goose.

I hold the money out to Thomas, who takes it from me silently. He puts the reins in one hand and counts the coins on his palm.

'Don't you trust me?' I ask quietly.

He puts the coins in his pocket. 'Thomas Walters trusts nobody,' he says.

13

I hardly see Thomas over the next few days. He starts work while it is still pitch-black outside and he comes in too late for supper. He makes sure that there is food in the larder and logs in the woodshed, but we do not eat together and we do not sit side by side in front of the fire. Sometimes I watch him from the window, chopping wood or hammering at the stable roof. What does he think about all day? I look for the sparkle of warmth beneath his scowl, gentleness in hands that wield the pitchfork, the axe . . . I know there is more to him than this – there are such stories in his dark eyes, but he will not share them with me. He has decided that he cannot trust me, that we have nothing in common. He thinks I am more like Clarence Asquith than I am him.

I sometimes think about Clarence describing Thomas as a 'common thief' and wonder how there can be any truth in it. When he goes to the market in Penrith or Carlisle, I imagine him tunnelling beneath the streets to break into the bank vault, and I almost laugh out loud – the idea of Thomas as a bank robber is ludicrous, comical. If he really were a criminal, he would commit a quiet, careful sort of crime – like forging oil paintings, or prising diamonds from necklaces. I've read about things like this.

Could he be my father? He would have been very young. He can't be much more than thirty now – his hair is thick and dark, his forehead is smooth. He must have been no more than eighteen or nineteen when I was born. Too young and too poor to raise a child. Perhaps he and my mother – whoever she was – left me on the steps of Gosswater Hall one winter's morning, swaddled in a white blanket, tucked into a basket. Perhaps the countess found me there and sobbed at the sight of such a little thing all alone in the world. Perhaps she took me into the house and fed me warm milk, and then couldn't bear to hand me over to the orphanage.

Yes. Something like that. The romance of such a start in life is oddly appealing – like a fairy tale – and I daydream about it as I sit by the fire day after day. I think about my real mother and try to remember the feeling of being held, being loved, but there is nothing like that in my memory at all. What happened to her? Did she move away from Gosswater? Did she die?

I watch the red-hot edge of heat spread through one log at a time, transforming wood to ash. As the clock in the parlour ticks the last hours of the year away, I embroider flowers on an old tablecloth. I mend a hole in my warmest shawl. I read the first act of *Hamlet*, with the ghost of the murdered king . . . I think about going ghost-watching with Bryn Black and wonder if I have the nerve after all.

Before I know it, it is New Year's Eve. It feels like any other grey winter's day to me. I don't think the rain cares that it is the last day of the century. The clouds hug the fells and the rain pours down. It thunders on the roof, finger-taps the windows, trickles in the gutters. I always feel sorry for the sheep when it is like this. I watch them from the upstairs windows, gathered together in soggy woollen masses, dripping and miserable.

At least you're not a sheep, Aggie, my brain says.

The seconds and minutes and hours go by. Tick. Tick. Tick. On the face of the parlour clock, just beneath twelve, there is a little panel with a dark blue disc that turns more slowly than the hour hand. At night-time a sleeping moon slides into view, and every morning it rotates to show a smiling sun with wavy yellow arms. I watch the painted sun slide slowly away. It is the only sun I've seen today. I put another

89

log on the fire and allow myself a wistful minute remembering the fireplace in my room at Gosswater Hall – the warmth of the blaze, the size of it – as grand as a cathedral; the basket of logs that was always – magically – filled. I sweep the cinders from the cracked hearth tiles, and go back to reading *Hamlet*.

The panel on the clock remains plain blue for an hour or two, but I know the sleeping moon is on its way. I must decide whether or not I am going to the island.

It is still raining. Well, that's a good enough reason not to go, I think. That and the idea of creeping around a cemetery in the middle of the night waiting for a decomposed duke to leap from his grave.

But Bryn dared you, Aggie, my brain says. *Dares are the sorts of things friends do, and it would be nice to have a proper friend.* Then it whispers, *And you like his red hair, don't you? And his dimple when he smiles . . .*

'I don't,' I say out loud. But my brain doesn't believe me. I go to the parlour window, press my nose against it and go cross-eyed watching raindrops race and dribble down the dark glass.

If this is your idea of fun . . . says my brain. And it has a point. If I don't go to meet Bryn, I might well spend the next ten years of my life watching raindrops dribble down the window and embroidering tablecloths. I wrap the warm shawl around my shoulders, go out of the back door and take a few steps down the slope of the wet garden. The lake is as black as the night, but I can just make out a tiny yellow light moving across the water. *Bryn.* He is heading towards the bay at the bottom of the lane, by the old willow tree, where I said I would meet him. I imagine him waiting for me there. Waiting and waiting, and then giving up on me.

You should go, Aggie, my brain says.

So I do.

Thomas has gone to bed and the house is quiet. I put on my warmest clothes, deliberately choosing things that are old and worn. I don't want Bryn to realize his mistake about me – not yet. I feel quite sure that Aggie the housemaid might be able to have adventures that Lady Agatha Asquith could never have had. She certainly seems to make friends more easily.

I creep back down the stairs and use my candle to light the hurricane lamp that Thomas keeps by the front door. I check the time on the parlour clock. Half past ten. Bryn said he would collect me from the bay with the willow tree at eleven o'clock. The clock's sleeping moon is smug and yellow in the lamplight. *You ought to be in bed*, it says. I poke my tongue out at it, open the front door and look out into the dark yard. The rain is relentless and the air is forbiddingly cold. Am I really going to do this? Yes. Yes, I am. I close the door as quietly as I can, and set off. Then – almost immediately – I stop. Something is there, moving in the shadows. *Ghosts an' ghosts*, the voice of Sexton Black echoes in my head – *Nasty things seep an' creep* . . . But I haven't made it to the island yet, and there is still over an hour until midnight. *Come on, Aggie* . . . Something moves again – a flash at the corner of my eye – and I turn quickly. *Fox?* It must be.

'So you survived the hunt, Fox,' I say out loud, and I'm glad. I hold up the lamp, hoping to see his luminous eyes, his white-tipped tail . . .

But it isn't Fox at all. A ghost-white shape emerges from behind a bale of straw, and hisses at me. 'Susan!' I gasp. 'You wretched thing – you scared the life out of me. Come on, quickly, back to your shed. How did you get out this time?'

But she won't be herded.

'Fox will get you, Susan,' I warn.

She dodges my arms and flaps at me crossly.

'Fine,' I say. 'But if you don't go in now, you'll have to wait until I get back.'

She hisses rudely and waddles away to investigate an old grain sack.

After this false start, I give myself a stiff talking to and make my way quickly out on to the lane, down the hill and along the dirt track to the shore of the lake. Bryn is already there, waiting for me in his rowing boat. The old willow tree is doing its best to protect him from the rain.

'I knew you'd come,' Bryn says with a dimpled grin.

'I nearly didn't.'

'Too good a chance t' miss – bit of an adventure wi' a handsome chap like me.'

I shake my head at him, smiling as he helps me into the boat.

The rain seems to be easing and, as we set off across the lake, it stops altogether. The clouds must be empty at last. The steady pattering is replaced by stillness and silence. The sky is starting to clear and I glimpse the moon, startlingly bright through rags of torn cloud. I feel a flutter of excitement.

Bryn is rowing, checking over his shoulder every now and then to make sure we are heading straight for the island. His red hair is dark with rain. The next time Bryn turns around, the moonlight falls upon his face.

'Oh, Bryn! What happened?' His left cheek is purple and swollen.

He turns back and rows. One stroke. Two. Then: 'Sexton Black happened.'

'He hit you?'

'Aye.' He manages to grin again. 'Don't worry, Aggie – I'm fine.'

I knew there was violence in those terrible eyes.

'Will he be about tonight?'

'Naw – he'll be fast asleep by now. He were dead drunk already, and I put an extra slug o' whisky in his cocoa just to make sure.'

'Good.'

We don't talk for a while. It is so quiet I can hear the running of the water on the bottom of the boat. I look back, but I can't see Thomas's cottage at all. It is just possible to make out the shape of Gosswater Hall, though, further along the shore: little squares of light all in a row mark the windows on the ground floor. Clarence must be having a New Year's Eve party. I picture the chandeliers blazing in his newly renovated ballroom; I imagine the baroness in a swirling dress, the music playing . . . There is a dull aching in my gut – a longing for the world I have been cast out of. I let it ache for a moment longer, and then let it go. I am glad I am here on the moonlit lake, in a boat with a boy called Bryn. I am glad I am not sitting alone by the fire in Thomas's parlour or huddled beneath a blanket with only the King Stone for company.

Skelter Island slides towards us through the darkness and I feel that flutter of excitement again. Mother told me I was wild and wayward, but this is easily the wildest thing I have ever done.

'Can I row, Bryn?'

'I dunno, Aggie – can you?'

I roll my eyes. 'I mean, could you show me how to row, please?'

We shift places, with much giggling and wobbling. Bryn shows me how to hold the oars, lifting and dipping, lifting and dipping. He shows me how to lean forward and back, using my whole body to pull them through the water. It is hard at first – when I concentrate on what one oar is doing, the other one goes wrong; I can't get them both to behave at the same time.

'You'll get it.' Bryn smiles. 'Soon it'll be second nature. Watch out, Aggie, or we'll miss the jetty.' He takes hold of one oar and paddles so that the boat changes direction. 'One more stroke,' he says. 'Ease up, now – let her drift.'

The jetty meets us with a solid thump and water sloshes over the side of the boat. We are here.

Bryn grins at me. 'Ready t' go ghost-huntin', Aggie?'

'Ready.'

14

We follow a path through the trees, stepping over stumps and puddles and twisted tree roots. There is an uncanny dance of light – the glow of the moon and the flicker of the moving lantern make the bare branches around us into thin shadowy limbs that reach and stretch and snap and snatch. Our own shadows falter behind us, as if trying to drag us back to the boat. Some of the oldest graves have been forced open by tree roots thick as snakes; I try not to look at the gaps between the stones, try not to imagine what lies beneath us. *If they all arose from their graves, they would be a legion* . . . No, I mustn't think like that. It's all nonsense – the ramblings of mad old Sexton Black. I'm only here because Bryn dared me. It's a game, an adventure . . .

Something rustles through the dead leaves and I stop and gulp. Bryn just grins. 'A rat or something,' he says. 'Lots of 'em here on the island. Rats and bats . . .'

'Bats?' I look up, wrapping my arms across my chest.

'Don't worry, Aggie – they're all sleepin' now, but you should see 'em in the summer – thousands of 'em all dartin' about through the trees and over the lake like clouds o' black butterflies. Beautiful.'

I frown at him.

'They eat the insects over the water,' he says, as if that explains everything.

I've never really thought about what bats eat, and I've certainly never thought of them as beautiful.

'C'mon Aggie,' Bryn says, setting off again. 'We don't have long till midnight.'

'Where are we going exactly?' My voice sounds much braver than I feel inside.

'What about the new grave?'

I stop again and my heart thuds. *Father's grave?*

'No.'

'Why not?'

It's hardly the right time to tell Bryn the truth now. Anyway, Father may have been a cold and curmudgeonly old man, but I can't imagine him having a restless soul: he always enjoyed a nap.

'Sorry, Aggie – I forgot. You must've known the old earl.'

'I . . . Yes. I knew him.'

'We'll find some older ones, then.'

We reach the clearing in which the grandest tombs stand – the resting places of the wealthiest and most important Asquiths. There are earls and countesses here; lords who led us into battle and ladies who had tea with the queen . . . And they are all just dust. *Just dust.*

'We should do summat,' Bryn says. 'To summon the ghost.'

'Do we need to? Sexton Black seemed sure it would come of its own accord – creeping through the crack in time . . .'

He laughs. 'A bit of encouragement can't hurt.' He rummages in his pocket, but all he can find is a bit of old string and a ship's biscuit. 'What have you got?'

'Nothing. Oh – wait. This.' I pull the mother-of-pearl hand mirror out of my pocket and hold it out.

He raises his eyebrows. 'Bet that's worth a bob or two.'

'Will it help?'

'Maybe.' He grins. He places the mirror face-up on an old marble slab, so that it captures a square of the black branches and midnight sky above, then he takes a stone and scratches a shape around it. He opens his arms and calls in a low, soft voice, 'Sleepin' ghosties, phantoms near, time to rise up and *appear*!'

'Are you making this up, Bryn?'

He laughs again. 'Aye – o' course I am. C'mon now.'

He raises his arms and begins his chant once more, and I find myself joining in. It is as if the words are drawn out from somewhere deep inside me: 'Lonely spirit, restless soul,' I sing, 'come to right the wrongs of old.'

'Ooh – you're good at this, Aggie. That was proper spooky.'

Yes, I think. *It was . . .*

Then the church clock starts to chime. Midnight is just a few moments away. Bryn and I look at each other and, quite instinctively, we crouch down, obscuring ourselves behind a bramble bush, as if we are stalking game. Bryn's eyes are alight, and we giggle.

The chiming is dull and flat, one of the notes is missing. There is a pause.

This is the moment – the gap between today and tomorrow, between one year and the next, between the centuries. This is the crack in time through which something will creep . . .

Then the clock starts to sound the hours. I hold my breath. The chimes ring through the cold air, golden in the blackness – one, two, three . . . But nothing stirs. I look from one crumbling vault to another. No spectre is seeping between the stones. Four, five, six . . . No corpse is creeping through the darkness. Seven, eight, nine . . . I am still holding my breath. Ten, eleven, twelve . . .

Silence.

A clattering in the branches above makes my heart skitter and my hand flies to my chest.

'Wood pigeon,' Bryn whispers, putting a steady hand on my shoulder. 'Clumsy idiot probably fell off 'is branch.'

My breathing settles once more.

We watch the tombs. The minutes pass. I am staring so hard into the darkness that my eyes are stinging. My fingers and toes are so cold I can hardly feel them. I am starting to get pins and needles in my legs.

'Bryn. Let's go,' I whisper at last.

'Aye. Ah, well, no ghosts!' He laughs, and stretches. 'Still — it was fun, wasn't it?' He retrieves my mirror and passes it back to me.

'It was,' I say, but I am not disappointed that Bryn's 'ghosties' didn't appear. The blood prickles its way back into my calves as I stand up.

'This way,' Bryn says. 'I'll show you where I live.' He takes up his lantern and heads towards the church. 'I'm fairly relieved,' he goes on, 'that I don't have to eat your hat, Aggie. Though I notice you didn't risk wearin' it tonight.'

'Well,' I say, smiling back. 'It's my favourite hat.'

Instead of heading towards the main door of the church, we follow a well-worn path that runs down the side of the building, through patches of nettles, compost heaps and the blackened sites of old bonfires. Then I see that there is a rough stone shack attached to the back of the church – little more than a stable.

'You live here?'

'Home sweet home.' He manages an ironic grin.

Gardening tools lean against the cottage wall like propped-up drunkards. The front door is rotten and the hinges are broken. The light that comes from the grimy, cobwebbed window is jaundice-yellow. I peer in and see a bare room lit by one guttering candle.

Then – BANG. A face at the window – toothless, wild-eyed and hideous. I scream and back away, bumping into Bryn. His lantern falls from his hand and shatters loudly.

'Grandfather!' he gasps.

Bony hands press at the glass and the toothless mouth bellows, 'BRYN BLACK!' The wild, red eyes roll madly, the mouth spits with fury, and the hands thump on the filthy glass. 'WHAT are you DOIN' out there, BOY? WHO'S THAT with yer? I'll BEAT yer, BOY – I'll BEAT and BRAY yer to within an inch of yer WRETCHED life, yer wicked, WICKED BOY!' He moves towards the door.

Bryn comes to his senses. He springs away, pulling me after him, wrenching my shoulder. 'RUN!'

15

We stumble through the long grass and brambles; we find a path, our feet skidding across broken stones, splashing through puddles, sliding through mud. I look back over my shoulder, gasping for breath – Sexton Black is following us, lurching through the darkness. He is holding a pitchfork, waving it in the air like a trident; he is yelling something about purging the wickedness from Bryn's immortal soul.

'*Faster*, Aggie!' Bryn urges, but I can't go any faster.

Trees, tombs, mud, trees, bushes, tombs . . . blood pounding in my ears, my chest screaming for air.

'Wait! Bryn – here!' I yank him sideways, towards a tomb. I draw the rusty bolt back and Bryn helps me force the door. The heavy wood sticks and grinds against the stone. We squeeze in and push the door closed again. We are both gasping – panting. Our hands are flat against the smooth wood of the door. We listen.

'I'll flay yer ALIVE! I'll KILL yer this time – yer ungrateful little WRETCH, yer foul little . . .'

The footsteps stagger past.

The furious voice grows quieter.

Sexton Black has gone.

We slump on to the stone floor, breathing more easily now.

'Well, it seems that extra slug o' whisky didn't work,' Bryn says. It is very dark inside the tomb, but I swear I can hear a grin spreading across his freckled face. 'I'll have t' get my hands on summat a bit stronger next time.'

'Next time? Bryn, you've got to get away from him – he said he's going to *kill* you . . .'

'And he might well've done if he'd caught us. But he'll have forgotten all about it by the mornin'.'

'Really?'

'Aye. His drunken rages come and go. Don't worry about me, Aggie – I'm bidin' my time. I can usually duck away or hide. He got lucky wi' this one.'

The shadow of a hand moves up to his bruised cheekbone.

'What sort of grandfather is he anyway? Treating you like that.'

Bryn's voice is surprised. 'Oh – he's not really my grandfather. He makes me call him that. He adopted me from th' orphanage last year.'

So we're both stray cats, then – Bryn and I. I suppose I should feel lucky that I found a more comfortable home at Gosswater Hall than he did here on Skelter Island.

'As if I could be related to that mad old stoat . . .' Bryn snorts.

'He frightened me, Bryn.'

When he replies, his voice is different. 'Aye – he frightens me too. I've found the trick is t' remember that I'm stronger than him – on th' inside, I mean. Stronger and better. And I'll get away from him, don't worry. I'm cookin' up a plan.'

I smile at him in the darkness and I think he is smiling at me too.

'Now, then. Where on earth are we, Bryn?'

'The eastern side of the island, I think – near where I found you t' other day.'

Yes . . . Of course we are. And it is then that I realize: we are *exactly* where he found me on the day of the funeral.

We are inside the silvery tomb.

I touch the smooth wall and floor of the vault and move backwards, feeling my way along in the darkness – the silvery stone is ice-cold beneath my fingers. My hands discover a structure beside me, rather like a

stone table. I stand up carefully, feeling up, along . . .
There is something on the table: a long, cold box, as
smooth as marble. A stone coffin. My fingers shrink
back. And suddenly I can smell flowers – summer
blooms, roses . . . A cold shiver starts at the base of my
neck, shuddering through my whole body.

*Lonely spirit, restless soul, come to right the wrongs of
old . . .*

'Bryn?'

'Yes.'

'Did you just whisper that chant in my ear?'

'What? No – I'm over here.' His voice is several feet
away – back by the door.

I move towards his voice. 'You didn't . . . You didn't
touch my hand?'

'No, Aggie, I . . .' His voice falters. 'What is it?'

I am aware of something in the blackness behind
me, and suddenly I know that we are not alone in the
tomb.

Something else is in here with us.

I am too terrified to turn around.

I shove the door of the tomb open and we both spill
out on to the moonlit path.

'What's wrong, Aggie?' Bryn is saying. 'Did you see
summat in there?'

I stagger back, hands scrabbling in the mud and
stones, staring in horror at the open door of the tomb.
There is a light in there now – a weird, cold light – like

a Hallowe'en moon.

'What the *hell* is that, Bryn? Is this a trick? This had better not be a trick.'

'It's not a trick, Aggie, I swear! What is it? I can't see anythin'!'

I look again, and he is right: there is nothing there – no weird light, only darkness. We sit still on the wet mud, just staring at the gaping black mouth of the tomb. Nothing happens. After a minute or so, Bryn gets up, closes the heavy door and bolts it shut. 'Do you want t' go back t' the boat, Aggie?' he says. 'Shall I take you home?'

I nod and he pulls me on to my feet.

We walk back to the jetty, moonlight shining on the bark of the silver birches to mark our path. Thomas's hurricane lamp is there waiting for us in the boat and I am so relieved to see its unwavering light. We clamber into the boat. Bryn unties the rope, takes up the oars and pushes off from the jetty.

'Perhaps ghost-huntin' was a bad idea,' Bryn says after a while. 'Especially after that funeral t'other day. Skelter Island can get inside your head – play tricks on you.'

Was it my mind playing tricks on me? I could swear that I smelt flowers, heard a whispering voice, saw a strange, glowing light . . .

And then, like a flame kindled by my thoughts, I see something on the distant water. My heart thuds hard. I very nearly cry out, *Turn around, Bryn! Look!* But I don't. What if he can't see it? What if it disappears again? It looks like glimmering mist, the shimmer of starlight on the lake — opal-white. It is moving, as if blown by the wind, towards the brightly lit windows of Gosswater Hall.

It is a girl — the shape of a girl.

'Are you all right, Aggie?' Bryn says, looking at me hard.

I stare at the distant lights of Gosswater Hall.

'I'm all right,' I lie.

16

The first days of the twentieth century are remarkably like the last days of the nineteenth. But I feel different inside. I have seen something impossible, something terrifying and beautiful. *There are more things in heaven and earth, Horatio ...*

Sexton Black was right – something *did* creep through the crack between centuries, but it wasn't a murderous duke or a headless earl. It was a girl – a ghostly girl of light.

Who is she? I have been thinking about little else.

I wonder if, somehow, she is the girl I said goodbye to on the day of Father's funeral – Lady Agatha Asquith. My former self. I imagined her stepping away from me into the silvery tomb and now, by the weird magic of midnight and the mirror, she has become a separate soul – my ghostly, aristocratic twin.

Or perhaps she is the spirit of the silvery tomb itself: a girl who was *Beloved*. But I have no idea who that tomb belongs to, and I feel sure there is a connection between the ghost and me: Bryn couldn't see her, but I could. Something links us together – an invisible thread, stretching between us like spider silk.

She must be an Asquith ancestor, or she would not be entombed on Skelter Island – a restless soul resurrected as she was in girlhood and returning to 'right the wrongs' of her life. That phrase, that chant, keeps echoing in my mind. I wonder how she will go about righting those wrongs. The very idea of wielding such power makes me quake: *Justice!* my brain says hungrily, thinking of everything Clarence has taken from me. *Vengeance . . .*

Whoever the Ghost Girl is, I think about her all the time. I see her in the flames of the parlour fire, in the white-horse waves of the lake, in the dark clouds that gather over the fells. I think of her haunting Gosswater Hall – a young woman, all in white – drifting up the sweeping staircase, floating into Clarence's bedroom and scaring him out of his silk pyjamas.

One cold, windy morning, when I am at the kitchen sink, scraping bits of burnt bacon from the frying pan, there is a polite tapping at the front door.

It is Cousin Clarence. I check to see if he has

brought Brutus with him, but he hasn't – thank goodness. He has come alone on his big grey mare. She is waiting for him by the stable, her dappled flanks steaming in the freezing air. Clarence is leaning casually against the cottage wall. He taps at his boot with a riding crop. At his feet there is a large, bulky bag.

'Aren't you going to invite me in?'

'What do you want, Clarence?'

He smiles slowly. 'I've come to tell you a story, Agatha,' he says.

'A story?' My stomach tightens, instantly wary. *What game is he playing today?*

'Yes. A story. Once upon a time, a handsome young earl was showing his beautiful fiancée his most precious jewel – let's call it . . . the King Stone. A magnificent opal – unique and dazzling – the talisman of the young lord's reign. But when they went together to admire it, do you know what they found instead?'

'What did they find?' I ask, hoping my innocent expression is convincing.

'They found this.' Clarence pulls the black glass cigar bowl from the bulky bag, holds it up to my face so that I can see it closely, and then hurls it at my feet. It smashes on the doorstep into a thousand dark shards. I gasp, starting backwards.

Clarence smiles again.

'Poor Odelia nearly fainted with shock when we discovered the King Stone was missing. She wanted to notify the magistrate, but I managed to hold her off.' He leans towards me so that his nose is almost touching mine. 'We wouldn't want the *authorities* interfering in our business, would we, Agatha?'

I hesitate.

Hold your nerve, Aggie, my brain whispers. *That opal is yours! Even if the earl and countess did think of you as a stray cat, they would never have wanted Clarence to have everything, and they couldn't have borne the shame of you being penniless. Hold. Your. Nerve . . .*

'I don't know where the King Stone is, Clarence.' I say, looking him in the eye.

'You're lying. I want it back – I *need* it. Odelia is insistent that I find it, and the old opal too – the white one. She says I'll never be a proper Earl of Gosswater without it. Says she won't marry me until the curse is lifted . . .' His face twitches and he grinds his teeth.

'The *Queen* Stone?' My innocence is genuine this time. 'The Queen Stone went missing years and years ago – *nobody* knows where it is.'

'Don't they?' He is staring at me so hard I can barely breathe. 'You are more deceitful than I thought, Agatha. If I wasn't so infuriated, I'd be impressed with your audacity. You know *exactly* where the Queen Stone is.'

'I don't!'

'You *do*! It says so in the *blasted* will!' He rips the document from his pocket, opens it and finds the place. 'Blah, blah, blah . . . *The Queen Stone hereby* blah blah blah. *Although this is technically part of the Gosswater estate, I hope Clarence will choose to honour his uncle's last wish by allowing Agatha to keep this heirloom . . . I will tell her where to find it.*'

I gasp – I was right: Father *did* want me to have some kind of inheritance after all! 'He left me the Queen Stone? It's mine?'

'No. *Mine*.' He thrusts the paper at me and then stabs at it with his finger. 'If I "choose to honour my uncle's last wish", it says. And I don't *choose*, little cousin. It is part of the estate, and it is part of the Asquith shield. The heritage of the entire family is built upon that stone – Uncle Henry must have been mad as a coot if he thought he could leave it to you.'

I am trembling with rage, trying not to react to Clarence's foul words and his foul breath in my face. I want that piece of paper. 'Let me see it!' I demand. 'You didn't tell me he wanted me to have something. Let me *see*!'

He holds the will out of my reach. 'You little grabbing wretch!' He raises his riding crop – and then Thomas appears, striding round the side of the cottage.

'What are you doin' on my land, Asquith?'

'Ah, Walters.' Clarence's riding crop drops to his side. He puts the will back in his pocket.

'I heard something smash – what's goin' on?'

'Just a little accident.' Clarence gestures to the glittering splinters on the doorstep. 'I'm sure Cinderella, here, can sweep it up. Oh, no – Cinderella went from rags to riches, didn't she?' he sneers. 'And you're the other way round, Agatha!'

'What are you doin' here?' Thomas comes right up to the door and folds his arms.

'Actually, I've got a proposal for Agatha.' Clarence picks up the bulky bag at his feet and pulls out my best black silk dress. 'I wondered if you would be interested in a little exchange. I know your *father*, here, isn't interested in Asquith money . . .'

Thomas doesn't react.

'But you do like the finer things in life, don't you, Agatha?' Clarence goes on. 'And you must be missing them terribly. What do you say to a deal? This beautiful dress in return for the things I am looking for?'

He passes the dress to me. My fingers tingle and my chest aches. It is the one I was dreaming about on the way to the funeral, the one that feels like wearing midnight . . . But to give up the King Stone for a dress? Clarence must be mad! My hatred for him pulses in my veins, thick and strong.

'No, thank you,' I say slowly. 'I don't really need clothes like this any more, Clarence, and I'm afraid I can't help you find your . . . missing things.' I drop the dress in the mud at his feet.

Thomas raises his eyebrows.

The false smile slides from Clarence's face. 'That's how you want to play it, is it, Agatha?' he snarls, and his riding crop twitches and switches through the air.

Thomas darts forward, and grabs Clarence's arm before the riding crop can strike my face.

'Get off me!' Clarence barks. 'Unhand me, you thug!'

Thomas pulls Clarence closer. 'Leave. Agatha. ALONE,' he growls, and then gives him an almighty shove.

Clarence staggers backwards, steadies himself, then comes back at Thomas like a charging bull, but Thomas's fist is ready and it swings up sharply, cracking Clarence on the jaw. There is a stunned moment of silence. My heart thunders. Thomas's nostrils flare with each breath. Clarence spits blood on to the doorstep. When he looks up, his face is murderous.

'She's a thief!' he hisses, pointing a trembling finger at me and baring his teeth. He bundles up the dirty dress and stuffs it back inside the bag. He turns and walks unsteadily over to his horse, who is jerking her head up and down, spooked by the commotion. Clarence drags himself up into the saddle. 'The rotten apple doesn't fall far from the ROTTEN tree, does it, Walters?' he shouts, and kicks at the horse so sharply she twists and lurches straight into a canter.

Thomas and I stand there in the doorway until the clattering hooves of the grey mare fade into the distance and all we can hear is the blustering wind. I think he is going to ask me what Clarence was talking about, or why he accused me of being a thief, but he doesn't.

He looks up at the sky.

'There's a storm coming,' he says quietly.

17

Thomas gives George some extra hay and bolts him firmly into his stable. He closes the shutters on all the cottage windows, balancing on a ladder as the gale gusts around him. I fill up the trough in the goose shed with grain and make sure they have enough water. The geese fuss and flap around me, but I am getting used to them now and they are getting used to me – apart from Susan, that is. She has been even grumpier than usual since New Year's Eve, when she was locked out in the cold for hours and hours.

'It was your own fault, Susan,' I say. 'You are a very naughty goose.'

She clacks her black-tipped beak and hisses at me from her nest.

'Ssssweet dreams,' I hiss back. We will never be friends.

The wind almost rips the shed door from my hands as I try to shut it behind me. I throw my weight against the bottom half and slam the top part of the door as hard as I can, banging the catches into place. The babbling of the geese is smothered by the roaring of the wind. It is almost dark now, and there is a crazed wildness in the air; the black clouds surge across the sky like stampeding cattle and the trees of Skelter Island wave their bare, storm-torn branches in a frantic semaphore – HELP! HELP!

I hope Bryn is all right. I picture him in that stinking, rickety shack and pray that the storm is the only thing he has to worry about tonight: that Sexton Black is unconscious, snoring in a stupor.

I go to bed early and curl up beneath the covers, but sleep doesn't come. The storm is too loud – too rowdy. It rattles the shutters and shrieks across the chimney pot.

The hours of the night are black, loud, fierce. The storm gets stronger, and it feels as if our cottage is at the very heart of it. It rages round and round, hurling metal buckets about, sending broken branches crashing down into the yard. I think I hear the faint chimes of the parlour clock somewhere beneath the roaring – was that eleven o'clock, or was it midnight?

The shutters on my window rattle more and more

violently until at last the wind is victorious and they fly open, slamming against the stone walls of the cottage and then banging back against the window frame with such force that the glass explodes into the room. The storm charges in like a barbarian, yelling and bellowing and whirling weapons about its head.

It tears around the room like a lunatic creature, shrieking and howling through the jagged jaws of the window frame, and then She is there too – the ghost.

I scream.

In a moment Thomas is through my door and at my side. 'Aggie? Aggie!'

But I can't take my eyes away from the girl at the window – bright amidst the black pandemonium that spins around her. I am staring at her and she is reaching out to me with pale hands. Is this *her* storm, *her* pandemonium?

'What is it, Aggie?' Thomas shouts as I lean closer to the shattered window.

'Can you see her, Thomas?'

'See who?'

'The girl—'

But her pale shape is drifting and blurring now – ribbons of moonlight in the wind.

'What girl, Aggie?' He has taken hold of my hands.

I look at him, and I watch his face change, as if he has seen something in my eyes – an echo, a reflection, a trace of her.

Then he is at the window, stretching out into the wild night, searching . . .

But she has gone.

We do not speak of it the next morning. After the nightmarish storm, the weather is drizzly, grey, apologetic. We barely say a word over breakfast. There is something self-conscious about our silence – as if we have both revealed parts of ourselves we would rather have kept hidden. I think of the raw emotion that possessed Thomas's face as he looked out into the storm. For a moment, he was a different person from the surly, closed-up man I have come to know.

After breakfast we set about clearing up the broken glass from my bedroom floor, and I manage to slice my hand on a razor-thin sliver of window pane. Thomas cleans the cut very gently with boiled water and dresses it with strips of clean cotton. It is the first fatherly thing he has ever done for me, and I have to pretend my tears are from the stinging of the wound. He looks at me for a moment, his large hand covering mine.

'Never mind, lass,' he says quietly. 'You'll heal.'

I don't know if he means my hand or all the other things that are hurting too – the things that can't be seen.

He goes downstairs and comes back up with some bits of wood and the tool bag that was at the back of the kitchen cupboard. I watch while he sweeps up the remaining splinters of glass from the floorboards, then takes a hammer from the bag and starts to nail the wooden planks across the broken window. As he adds more planks, the cold little room gets darker and warmer.

'I'll go into Penrith tomorrow and get some glass t' fettle it properly,' he says, lining up another plank. I poke about in his tool bag, examining all the strange, sharp, shining things.

'Thomas . . .' I begin.

'Aye?'

'What Clarence said yesterday, about me being a thief . . .'

He interrupts me. 'You don't have to tell me anythin', lass. It's your own business.'

'It's not theft if you are entitled to take something, is it? If something is owed to you?' I ask. 'It's a sort of . . . justice, isn't it?'

'Justice . . .' Thomas murmurs darkly. 'That's a tricky one. I wouldn't know much about justice.' Then: 'But I do know about the truth, and I know I'd take your word over Clarence Asquith's any day.'

'Thank you,' I say quietly, unsure I fully deserve his confidence.

'I don't trust that man any further than I could throw 'im,' Thomas mutters.

I can't help smiling: 'That's quite a long way,

though, Thomas,' I say, 'if yesterday was anything to go by.'

'Ha!'

I've never made him laugh before. I can feel that spark of friendship again – that tiny, bright flame. And yet we know so little about each other. I wish I could talk to him properly, tell him about all the phantoms spinning in my head – Father's dying breaths; Great-aunt Millicent's haunted face; Sexton Black chasing me through my nightmares; the King Stone hidden in my bed; the hatred for Cousin Clarence that is growing like a cancer inside me; and – most of all – the Ghost Girl that only I can see. But I know that I can't share these things with him. Not yet.

I decide to say something different instead. 'What are these tools for, Thomas?' I am holding a tiny chisel and a strange, hooked blade.

He turns around. 'I used to be a carpenter, Aggie.'

Not the tools of a thief, then. A carpenter makes sense, I think – given his well-maintained little cottage, the perfectly aligned planks nailed snugly across the window.

'I worked on some of the churches round these parts, buildin' pulpits, pews. I did wood-carving too – patterns, pictures, letterin' from the Bible. People liked my work.' He reaches out for the tiny chisel. 'I haven't done it for years now, though. Not since . . .' He stops and a shadow passes across his face.

'Can you show me?'

'What?'

'What you do – carving the wood.'

'I . . .' He looks at the little chisel again, then he looks at me. 'It's been a long time . . .'

'Please.'

He picks up a small hammer, and then turns to the boarded window. 'It's not the right sort o' wood, o' course . . .' He looks at the plank for a moment, and then places the chisel very carefully. He taps it softly with the hammer, moving it, placing it and tapping again. He blows the shavings away. He taps and blows and taps and I start to see a face emerging from the rough timber – two almond eyes, a narrow muzzle . . . Thomas works with the grain, using the natural lines and knots and swirls of the wood – and it is like witchcraft: there was nothing, and now there is something – something alive looking right back at me. Its eyes glisten. The fur bristles. I can almost see it breathing.

'Somethin' like that,' Thomas says, looking at his work for a second, before cleaning his tools and putting them back in the bag. He sweeps the wood shavings into the same dustpan as the glass shards.

'It's beautiful,' I say, breathless. 'Just beautiful, Thomas. It's Fox!'

A smile spreads shyly across his face; his eyes crinkle and sparkle. He looks so different – handsome, happy.

'You should go back to it.'

The smile fades gently and he looks down. 'No,' he says at last. 'It's all . . . too long ago.' Suddenly, his eyes are swimming and sparkling.

He is thinking about more than just his work . . . I remember the petals I found in that envelope, the lock of golden hair.

'Thomas?'

'Aye?' He wipes his eyes with the back of his hand and stands up.

'Tell me about her – please. About my mother.'

He takes a long breath and swallows. 'I will, lass. Not today, though. Not right now, eh?' He moves towards the door and my heart sinks.

I am still struggling to digest this truth I have been served up: that I am the daughter of Thomas Walters, the goose farmer. There has been a great chasm between us: the gulf between his world and my own. But somehow we have begun to find a way towards each other. I *like* him – I just don't understand how he is my father. I need to know my own story. If only he would tell me . . . But he is going down the stairs now. 'I'll be out in the barn if you need me,' he calls.

I look at the carving of the fox face, trying to distract myself from the floodwater of feeling that is rising within me. I reach out and touch it, feeling the artistry in each tiny scoop of wood. I look at Fox. And Fox looks at me. Something prickles in the back of my mind: this carving reminds me of something – a dream? A memory? A thing half-forgotten. I close my eyes and try to connect the two things in my head, but they are so similar they push away from each other like magnets. No. I will have to wait for the memory to find me in its own good time.

18

The cut on my hand means I am excused from chores and Thomas takes over the kitchen. It is quite something to eat bacon that tastes like bacon, and toast that isn't charcoaled. The following morning, while we are eating our bacony bacon and unburnt toast at the kitchen table, Thomas opens a letter. He reads it several times, a deep frown on his face. Then he puts it back inside the envelope.

'What is it?' I ask. I am worried it is something legal, something to do with me. Perhaps Clarence has informed the police about me after all, or about Thomas punching him . . . *No, Aggie – the police wouldn't send a letter, would they?*

'It's about a job,' Thomas says. 'At the church in Penrith.'

'A carpentry job? Wood-carving?'

'Aye.'

I nod and wait.

'It's a job I started years and years ago,' he says. 'I carved the pews and gallery with animals from the Bible – donkeys, sheep and oxen, whales and lions, and all Noah's animals two by two.'

I smile, imagining those creatures coming to life under Thomas's hand.

'But then I – I couldn't finish it, and, t' be honest, I'd forgotten all about it until now. The minister says he'd like me to finish the job. He's just had a large donation for the upkeep of the church, so he says he could pay me a good wage to do the remaining pews. He'd like to get it done soon, before a grand service the bishop's plannin'.'

'Do you want to do it?'

'I . . . I don't know. It'll mean travellin' to Penrith, long days away, stayin' overnight perhaps.' He shakes his head. 'I can't leave you here to cope on your own, lass.'

'You can,' I say. 'My hand is healing well, and I can look after the geese by myself now.'

He looks at me earnestly. 'Are you sure? I mean, we could do wi' the money . . .' He takes the letter out of the envelope and reads it once more.

'I'm sure.' I hadn't thought about the financial strain on Thomas with an extra mouth to feed. It hadn't even crossed my mind. 'You should do it, Thomas,' I say firmly.

Thomas is packing his tools into the cart. He says he will be back very late tonight – he has sent word to the minister that he is coming, and that he can start work straight away. He seems nervous but cheerful, and I am glad I helped him to make up his mind.

'Are you sure you're all right for me t' go, Aggie?'

'Yes. Don't worry about me, Thomas, please.'

'Last chance to change your mind,' he says, checking George's harness.

I laugh: 'I'll be fine!'

An icy wind blasts dead leaves through the yard and George skitters sideways.

'Weesht, George,' Thomas says. 'Cush, cush. Ea-sy boy, stand now.' He climbs into the cart and takes up the reins.

'Goodbye!' I call after them as the cart trundles through the gate and out on to the lane. Another gust of the icy wind, and I pull my shawl around my shoulders.

'I'll be fine,' I say again as I head back into the empty cottage.

It is a quiet day. I muck out George's stable and put a net of clean hay ready for him when he gets home tonight. I'm sure the poor pony will be exhausted after such a long day. I'll give him some warm oat mash in the morning – he loves that.

Later on, I feed the geese and make sure I herd them all back into the shed before it starts to get dark. I count them, checking Susan is definitely there before I shut them in. Then I open the door and check again. For once, she doesn't hiss at me. She clacks her beak softly, then fusses at her feathers and tucks her head under her wing.

I make a sort of stew with a rabbit Thomas caught, some vegetables that I find in the larder and a few frost-toughened herbs from the kitchen garden. I leave it simmering gently on the stove.

Just look at you, Aggie, my brain says. *Mucking out stables, herding geese, cooking stew. You couldn't have done any of this a few weeks ago.*

No. I couldn't. A few weeks ago, I was a different person altogether. I think about my new life here with Thomas. Since the storm, we are closer, easier in each other's company, but I know he does not fully trust me yet. If he did, surely he would tell me all the things I am so desperate to know – about his mysterious past, about my mother, and who I really am. I didn't know until now how fragile trust is: Thomas and I are taking such small, shuffling steps towards each other, always listening for the cracking and creaking of the ice beneath our feet. But I think it is very nearly a sort of friendship; I have seen his slow, crinkled smile several times now.

Thinking of smiles makes me think of Bryn Black and his broad, dimpled grin. I haven't seen him since New Year's Eve – a week ago now. I wrap my shawl around my shoulders, take a lantern and go out into the garden. It is dusk. The cold air sweeps down from the fells like a great white eagle, gliding over Gosswater and shivering the waves.

'Are you all right, Bryn?' I whisper, looking out towards Skelter Island. I hope he knows I am thinking of him. I hope he survived the big storm – and Sexton Black's drunken raging. I wish I had a way of contacting him. I am about to head back into the cottage when I see something moving on the surface of the lake – a tiny light and a dark shape with a wake of water behind. I walk down to the very bottom of the garden where the waves lap at the grass and Thomas's rowing boat is moored. I squint at the dark shape out on the lake until it becomes clearer, and a happy pang hits my heart.

'Bryn!' I shout. 'Over here!' But he can't hear me above the buffeting wind. I hold up my lantern and use my thick shawl to cover it, then I move the shawl back and forth so the light flashes. It takes a moment, but eventually his light flashes back in reply. I flash the lantern once more and shout again, 'BRYN!' and the little boat turns towards me. As he gets closer, I can make out his face, grinning and ruddy beneath a woollen hat.

'I were headin' for the jetty at Gosswater Hall,' he calls. 'Thought I'd sneak into the kitchens and find you, Aggie. What are you doin' here?' He throws me a rope.

'I live here.' I catch the rope and pull the boat in, tying it up to the iron loop that Thomas's boat is tethered to.

'You live *here*?'

'Yes. Watch out – it's boggy just there.'

He crouches and then makes an enormous leap from the boat, over the muddiest part of the bank, and lands right in front of me, skidding slightly in a pile of goose droppings.

I catch his arm to stop him falling over and we both laugh. It is a very dark, cold evening – but I suddenly feel warm and happy.

'You live here?' he says again, gesturing at Thomas's cottage.

I laugh again. 'Yes!'

'I thought you'd live-in at Gosswater Hall.'

Live-in? *Of course*, my brain pipes up. *He thinks you are a servant there, Aggie.*

'Oh, yes – well, I did live . . . at Gosswater Hall. But . . .'

'You don't any more?'

'No. I live here now. With Thomas. My father.' It's the first time I have said it out loud and it feels strange.

Not because I am ashamed to be his daughter, but because it feels as if I'm admitting defeat somehow. *If you accept that this is your lot, Aggie, then Cousin Clarence has won . . .*

'Thomas Walters, the goose farmer – he's your father?'

I hesitate. 'Yes. Do you know him?'

'Aye – I bump into him in th' village every now and then. Seems like a nice man. I didn't know you were his daughter.'

No, my brain says. *Neither did I.*

'Come on,' I say, changing the subject. 'It's freezing out here – let's go inside.'

'Aye.' As we walk towards the cottage, Bryn looks up and sniffs at the squalling sky. 'Smells like snow,' he says.

'What does snow smell like?'

'Well . . .' He thinks for a few seconds. 'When there's snow comin', the air smells like cold metal, and wet, too – but not clarty-wet, like rain – clean, bright-wet. White.'

'Snow smells white?'

'Are you laughin' at me, Aggie?'

'Yes, Bryn – I am.'

'Well, I can't say I blame you. I'm a very witty young man.'

I give him a shove.

'Don't suppose you've got a morsel to eat in there

'ave you?' Bryn says as we head for the kitchen door. 'I'm reet famished.'

'I'm sure I can find something . . .' I stop. 'Oh, Bryn! The stew!'

19

I fly into the kitchen where the rabbit stew has bubbled down into a thick, brown mess and is catching on the pan.

'Oh! It's all burnt on the bottom. It's ruined.'

'Don't worry! I've sorted worse messes than this,' Bryn says. 'We'll let it cool for a minute. Bring me a clean pan and a wooden spoon – and a bit o' butter. Has this kettle got hot water in it?' He ladles and stirs, adds water and stirs again. He asks me what we have in the larder. He adds a bit of this, a bit of that. Eventually, he tastes it and is satisfied. He offers me the spoon. It is delicious – rich and meaty and warming.

'Not a trace of burnt bottom!'

'What can I say?' Bryn grins. 'I'm a man o' many talents.'

I leave a good helping in the pan for Thomas, and spoon the rest of it into bowls. Bryn and I sit by the parlour fire and eat. I watch him shovelling the stew into his mouth with great handfuls of bread. He really was hungry.

'When will your father be back then?' he asks between mouthfuls.

'I don't know. Late, he said.'

He nods. 'D'you have brothers or sisters? Will your mother be cross about me eatin' the stew?'

'I don't have brothers or sisters. I don't have a mother. It's just me and Thomas here.'

Bryn looks at me steadily and nods again. He cleans his bowl with a big chunk of bread, and then chews on it thoughtfully.

'Did she die?'

'My mother? I don't know. I don't know who she was.'

'Me neither,' says Bryn. 'My earliest memory is scrumpin' apples in an orchard – I were too little to climb the wall with t'other boys and I got caught. Instead of beatin' me, the old gardener and his wife took me in. I lived with them for a few years. They were nice folk – taught me to read and write and cook, how to look after animals, too. Closest thing I've ever had to a real home. When they died I came to the town lookin' for work, but the countess saw me on the street and told me I were too young to be fendin' for myself, so she took me to th' orphanage.'

Mother. 'The countess?'

'Aye – stuck-up posh old busybody. Did you know her, or was she before your time at the Hall?'

I try not to flinch. 'I knew her.'

Posh. Doesn't he think my voice is posh compared to his? Perhaps he thinks all housemaids talk like me . . .

I decide to change the subject. 'What was it like? At the orphanage?'

Bryn takes a long breath. 'Let's just say I'd have been better off on the streets.' He looks me in the eye to make sure I understand. Then he takes the poker and jabs at the fire. Fresh flames leap up. 'Have you ever asked Thomas about her?'

My brain flickers, confused. 'About the countess?'

'About your mother.'

Keep up, Aggie. 'Sort of. I think he finds it difficult to talk about.'

Bryn nods again. Perhaps he understands Thomas better than I do.

'If you think you were born around here, there's someone else you could ask,' Bryn says. 'Old Moll, the midwife. Lived in Gosswater village and delivered babies for over fifty year. Delivered lambs too. All the farmers sent for Moll if they had a sheep that were strugglin'. She never lost a lamb, nor a baby. But she left the village years ago – come into money and bought th' old folly on Thorn Island at north end o' the

135

lake. Lives there all by herself.'

'And you think she might know who my mother was?'

'If she delivered you, she'll know. People say she's a bit of a witch. Old as the hills, and blind as a bat.'

'Blind?'

'Completely blind now.'

'How does she manage all on her own?'

Bryn shrugs. 'She gets food delivered by boats from the village – I've seen Ivy, the baker's daughter, goin' up to Thorn Island in her skiff. I think she's her niece or summat. Though people say the Speedwells haven't spoken a word to Moll since she become wealthy.'

The Speedwells?

'Her name is Moll Speedwell?'

'That's right.'

It was the name Clarence mentioned to the solicitor. It sounded like he was trying to get his hands on her money. Someone should warn her about him . . .

'Can we go and see her – Old Moll?'

'We can try. She might not want to see us, though. No one has really seen Old Moll since she moved to Thorn Island. Rumour is, she took some sort o' vow to live apart. Like a hermit, or a nun.' He sees the disappointment in my face. 'But we can try,' he says again.

We sit quietly for a while. Bryn puts another couple of logs on the fire and it crackles happily.

'I like it here,' he says. 'I'd give anything for a

home like this.'

I look around Thomas's parlour, seeing it in quite a different way – the whitewashed walls, the comfortable chair big enough for me to curl up in, the worn red rug on the floorboards, the softly ticking clock above the fireplace. *Is this what home feels like?*

'I should go back soon,' Bryn sighs, and I watch reflections of firelight dancing in his eyes – hazel and gold. 'There'll be hell t' pay if I'm not there when he wakes up.'

But the wind is wuthering. 'It'll be a horrid journey home, Bryn – rowing back in this weather.' Then I have an idea: 'Don't go back. Stay here with me and Thomas – we can ask him if it's all right when he gets home later.'

Bryn looks up. He is thinking about it. 'Maybe . . .' he says. 'I'm sure I could make myself useful – I could help with th' geese.'

'And the pony. Perhaps you could do deliveries in the cart?' We are both grinning now. The fire pops with excitement.

'D'you think he might say yes?'

'I don't know.' And I really don't. I don't know Thomas well enough yet to guess his reactions to anything.

'I don't want to go back there, Aggie,' Bryn says. And I think I see him shudder. 'It's not just Sexton Black. It's the island. Since New Year, the place feels different somehow. Fearsome.'

We haven't spoken about what happened at New Year until now. I am glad it was Bryn who mentioned it first.

'I find myself watchin' for things movin' between th' tombs,' he says. 'I keep checkin' over my shoulder. And every time a duck quacks, I jump a foot into the air.' We both laugh, but then he looks at me – deadly serious. 'What was it you saw, Aggie?'

Can I tell him the truth? Will he think I'm mad – like Sexton Black? I open my mouth to speak, unsure of what is about to come out, but then something stops me – a noise outside the cottage. A scuffling – just under the parlour window.

'What's that?' We both listen. It is hard to make anything out above the sound of the wind.

'It's probably nothing,' I say.

'A fox?'

But then there is a louder noise – another scuffle, and a substantial thump. We look at each other.

'That's not a fox,' says Bryn. He goes to the window, peering through the curtains into the dark yard. 'I was right about the snow. It's blizzardin' down – there's a good inch or so on the ground already . . . And, Aggie—' His voice has changed.

'Yes?'

'There are footprints in the snow. Right across the yard. Someone's here.'

Footprints? 'Well, it can't be Thomas . . . ' Then a ghastly thought occurs to me. 'You don't think it could be Sexton Black, do you, Bryn? Could he have followed you here?'

'I hope not, I—'

We both jump as the front door suddenly rattles violently.

Someone is trying to get in.

20

'Quick, Bryn – up the stairs.'

We scuttle from the parlour and up to my room. The rattling of the door grows louder, and then there is a heavy thud and a creak, as if someone is trying their weight against it.

We crouch in the darkness behind my bed. I notice a sliver of glass glinting up at me from between the floorboards – a fragment of the broken window that we missed. A shame it's not big enough to be used as a weapon. My brain skitters about in a panic – I am looking for something we can defend ourselves with – and there is only one thing I can think of. I slide my hand between the cool sheets of my bed, up and under my pillow, and my fingers close gratefully around the cold, hard shape of the King Stone.

One last thud against the door below, and then it goes quiet again. Perhaps they have given up. I thank goodness that Thomas is a carpenter: the front door is sturdy, the lock is strong. It only takes a moment for me to realize the horrible significance of the silence, and by then it's too late: 'Bryn – the back door!'

A burst of louder weather as the door clicks open and closed, and then footsteps across the flagstones of the kitchen.

The intruder is inside the house.

Whoever-it-is must be in the parlour now, taking in the empty bowls, the burning candles, the crackling fire. They know we are here somewhere.

I grip the King Stone tightly in one hand, and grasp Bryn's arm with the other. The footsteps are coming up the stairs – heavy but careful. There is the sound of laboured breathing too. When the footsteps reach the top of the stairs, they pause. Left or right?

The other way, I pray silently. *Go the other way.* And they do – they go down the landing towards Thomas's room.

'*Now*, Bryn,' I whisper. And I spring up, leading the way, leaping down the stairs four at a time, spinning through the kitchen door and out into the snow. Bryn is right behind me. I had half a thought to run all the way down the garden and get into his boat, but we couldn't get far enough from the shore; we'll have to hide. I open the door to the goose shed and we both dash in. I manage to fasten the catch on the bottom half of the door and pull the top half back firmly, hoping the catch will swing into place. The geese are startled and begin chattering and flapping about in the darkness. 'Shhh,' I say. 'It's me. Shhh, girls!'

I remember Thomas's words when he first introduced me to the geese – *as good as guard dogs*. I pray that they will keep us safe. It is not quite pitch-black in here: rays of moonlight have found their way through a small, dusty window and through chinks in the old roof, diluting the darkness.

'Over here, Bryn.' I grope through the gloom, heading for the furthest corner of the shed behind the clean bales of straw. We can use the pitchfork if we need to, and I've still got the King Stone clutched in my hand, ready to hurl at the attacker's head . . . The geese are settling themselves and, for a moment, everything is quiet. Then, from somewhere outside, near the back of the cottage, there is a voice.

'Agatha,' it calls, low and sinister. And, immediately, I know who it is.

'Clarence,' I breathe in horror. I didn't think he would come back here after Thomas sent him packing – I didn't think he'd *dare*. But Thomas isn't here now . . . Has Clarence been watching the cottage? Waiting for the best moment to come back and . . .

'Oh, God,' I whisper. 'Bryn – take this – quickly!' I press the King Stone into his hand.

He squints at it for a moment, then his eyes open wide with surprise.

'Aggie – what on earth? Did you *steal* this from Gosswater Hall?'

'No, I . . . Sort of. It's mine now.'

Bryn opens his mouth to say something, but he just stares at the opal instead. The stone glimmers at us – a perfect, gleaming droplet of darkness. It knows it is beautiful; it knows it is dangerous. *Clarence is not going to get his hands on it. It is MINE.*

'I need you to look after it, Bryn – please. He mustn't find me with it. I'll explain later.'

Bryn swallows. He looks at me. 'Wait here,' he says. He gets up and tiptoes towards the other end of the shed, where the geese have settled again. He is heading straight towards Susan. She gets to her feet and beats at the air with her wings. I am about to warn him not to go any closer, but then something peculiar happens. Bryn raises both of his arms. He stretches his head forwards and stares straight at Susan. *I am a bigger goose than you*, he seems to be saying. Susan clacks her beak shut and tilts her head to one side, looking at him comically. Then she dips her head and tucks her wings back against her body. Bryn drops his 'wings' too. He walks slowly past Susan and places the King Stone in the straw where she was sitting.

'Look after this for Aggie,' he whispers.

She waddles back, taps the opal with the black tip of

her beak, rolls it about a bit, and then settles down on it as if it were her own egg. The soft white feathers of her belly nestle around the black jewel and hide it from view.

If it wasn't for the heavy footsteps that are heading towards the goose shed, I might have applauded. 'Amazing,' I breathe.

He shrugs. 'I told you – I'm good wi' animals.' He creeps back and I grab at the silhouette of his hand, pulling him down next to me – and just in time: fingers are scratching at the catches of the shed door.

'Agatha,' the voice calls, horribly soft. 'Lady Agatha?' Both halves of the door swing open at once and a cold white light floods in – moonlight reflected by the snow. 'I know you're in here,' the voice says. 'I followed your footsteps in the snow – you silly goose. Have you got a friend in here with you? Has my silly little cousin made a silly little friend?' There is another sound alongside his voice – a heavy panting, the click of claws on the floor of the shed.

Brutus. My stomach twists and I have to swallow a mouthful of sour stew.

'I'm not going to hurt you, Agatha,' Clarence chuckles. 'Not unless I have to. I just need you to give me the opals . . .'

He stops. Everything goes quiet, and then I hear a low hissing noise that gets louder and louder until it sounds like jets of scalding-hot steam. I dare to peek around the straw bales. *Goodness!* The geese have surrounded Clarence and his dog – a gaggle of angry white harpies – every single one of them pointing her beak and hissing in rage.

Brutus growls, but steps backwards, unnerved.

'Go away, you stupid birds!' Clarence shouts, lashing at the geese with his riding crop.

What a terrible mistake. They all rush at once – fifty pairs of wings raised, fifty long necks stretched out like the snake-heads of the Hydra. They have become a huge, surging white wave, drowning Clarence and his cowering dog.

'Aargh!' Clarence yells. 'Aaaargh! Get off! Get OFF!' But the more he swings his crop at them, the more violently they attack.

He backs out of the shed, Brutus crawling at his heels in terrified submission; then they run, and the geese pursue them into the blizzard, wings flapping, beaks clacking and hissing.

I slump down in the straw. 'Extraordinary!' I say, breathing properly for what feels like the first time in half an hour. I almost laugh. 'Remind me to tell you the legend of the Queen Stone one day, Bryn . . .'

Bryn is silent. I lift my head and find him staring back at me coldly. His eyes flash.

'*Lady Agatha?*' he says. '*Cousin?* That was *the earl*, Aggie! That was the new Earl o' Gosswater callin' you cousin! You told me *Thomas* was your father! You let me think . . .' He gets to his feet and glares at me. His eyes are glinting with angry tears. 'You're an Asquith! You're one o' *them*!'

'No, Bryn – it's not as simple as that,' I stammer – and the fear of losing my only friend is suddenly much, much worse than the fear of Clarence and his dog. 'I . . .'

But he is making for the door.

I haul myself to my feet and follow him. 'Bryn – WAIT!'

He is halfway down the garden already. He stops and turns: a thin black figure in the snow – a lonely letter on a page. 'Who *are* you, Aggie?' he shouts. 'Who the *hell* are you?'

The wind gusts, hurling huge snowflakes into my eyes, my mouth. What can I possibly say?

21

It takes for ever to round up all the geese, chasing their white shapes through the snow and shepherding them into the shed. I stumble back into the cottage, my fingers and toes burning with cold, and I gasp. The kitchen has been ransacked. Every cupboard has been turned out, every drawer rummaged through. I walk through the rest of the house in a daze. Every room is the same.

Well, perhaps Clarence will actually believe that I don't have the King Stone now ...

By the time I have tidied up, locked up and got myself into bed, it is very late. I know Thomas will not be driving home in this weather. For the first time in my life, I am to be alone in a house for an entire night – no one snoring down the corridor, no servants snoozing in the attics above. I huddle down beneath the bed clothes, exhausted. I close my eyes and wait for sleep . . .

It refuses to come.

The snow-heavy wind is beating against my window, but all I can hear is Bryn's voice – colder than the blizzard: *Who* are *you, Aggie?*

I turn over, open my eyes and close them again. I pull the blanket up over my head.

Who the hell *are you?*

The parlour clock strikes midnight – twelve clear, high chimes – and it feels like an answer to Bryn's question. I am midnight. Neither one day nor the next. Yesterday is behind me, and a new dawn is ahead. But right now there is only darkness . . .

It is late morning when I wake up, and it is still snowing. The whole world beyond my window is white. Each rock, each bush, each treetop is draped with a cloak of ermine. The shallows of the lake have frozen, and snow has settled on the ice and on the clumps of reeds, making the lake look smaller and rounder – fringed with white. I'll keep the geese in the shed today and give them some extra grain. Susan can keep watch over the King Stone for me.

And it is only then that I think about Thomas. *Could* he have come back? His bedroom door is standing open. Nothing seems to have been touched since I tidied it up last night. His unslept-in bed answers me with an insolent stare.

No. He has not come home. With such heavy snow, he will have been forced to stay in Penrith last night, and he will have to remain there until Ramskull Pass is open again. I remember crossing the pass in a carriage with the countess, the earl and Miss McCarthy when I was six or seven. We were going to the church in Penrith for the Christmas service. There was a little snow on the ground, and the driver had to take the journey very slowly so the horses didn't slip. It felt like hours and hours, winding up that steep, treacherous road all the way to the summit. Miss McCarthy pointed out of the window, showing me the huge sheep's skull lodged there on a fence post: all that was left of the legendary ram who roamed the fells for generations: *Beware*, he bleats through the darkest, coldest nights. *Beware!*

And Thomas is no fool – he will have heeded the old ram's warning. I think of poor George and hope that Thomas managed to find him a nice warm stable for the night.

I light a fire and make myself some porridge. I feel numb, strangely detached from everything that has happened. It is as if the snow has settled over my mind as well as the world outside – my thoughts are deadened, muffled. Do I feel lonely? Afraid? I ought to – I am completely alone now. I try on different feelings, but nothing quite seems to fit. Am I sad about the argument with Bryn? Am I angry with Thomas for abandoning me just when I was starting to feel safe? Am I frightened that Cousin Clarence will come back? It is as if all these feelings have been used up, but I have found something else instead – a calmness at my very core. A cool, warrior-like determination: I have nothing more to lose; I am ready for battle. And I know exactly where I must start.

I pull on my warmest boots, wrap my scarf around my neck, and lock the back door behind me. The clouds are grey and heavy but, for the moment, no more snowflakes are falling from the sky. The fresh snow crunches and squeaks pleasingly beneath my boots as I step, step, step down the garden. Snow-cold air rushes into my nose, my lungs, and it is like breathing in something completely new. I feel excited. Alive. At the bottom of the garden, the boggy patch of grass has frozen. The ice snaps and splinters under my weight. I tread carefully, grabbing the side of Thomas's rowing boat and rocking her to and fro to free her. I untie her, climb in, and use an oar to push myself off from the bank. Gravel grinds against her hull, weeds tear and ice cracks, but soon the little boat is rocking gently on the cold, still water, and I take up the oars.

I had a strange dream last night – not a nightmare, but a soft, white dream that shimmered through me, warm as milk. There was a song made of light, and words that were just thoughts, melting like snowflakes: *Moll Speedwell, Moll Speedwell, the witch of Thorn Island* . . . Old Moll has been in my head since the moment I woke up: she is part of this puzzle somehow. Clarence is trying to get his hands on her money and – according to Bryn – she might be able to tell me who my mother is. Why should I wait for him to take me to Thorn Island when I am perfectly capable of getting there myself?

I sniff, straighten my back, grit my teeth and grip the oars.

I count the strokes under my breath – five, twenty, forty, a hundred; finding a rhythm helps me to keep the oars together. Sometimes they catch or splash or skim the water instead of dipping, but the boat keeps moving steadily. Each stiff pull takes me further north – further from Thomas's cottage, further from Goss-water Hall.

My arms are aching. I rock backwards and forwards from my hips, trying to make each stroke as long and strong as possible. I am passing Skelter Island now. I fight the urge to look – to see if Bryn is there on the jetty, waving both arms at me, calling for me to stop and take him with me. I glance very quickly, hoping my brain won't notice – but he is not there. I pull up the oars for a moment to rest my arms, and just allow the boat to drift. Shrouded in snow, the spindly trees and church spire of Skelter Island look like ghastly sculptures made with the bones of the dead. I notice a ghost of smoke rising up from behind the church, and imagine Bryn and Sexton Black sitting beside a miserable little fire in cold silence.

I take up the oars again. The brass rowlocks creak, complaining. My arms are complaining too, and my fingers and palms, which have started to blister beneath my gloves. They are not used to this sort of thing.

Never mind, lass. You will heal.

I settle back into a rhythm again. My brain starts singing – 'Amazing Grace' – in time with the rowing. I breathe through each stroke, blowing plumes of steam into the freezing air.

How sweet
The sound
That saved
A wretch
Like me . . .

The oars creak in time, the water splashes. I am warm now. And I am far beyond Skelter Island. I have never been up to this far end of the lake. I can see no houses, no roads or tracks or even footpaths – everything is rock and shale and scrub. No one lives here apart from the birds and – apparently – old Moll Speedwell.

At last an island starts to take shape in the distance. As I get closer, I can see that there is a building on it: an odd little castle – a folly built of grey stone, with battlements and a pointed turret. That must be where Moll lives, but – I almost laugh – it is a ludicrous place to live – like something from a storybook. Each pull draws me nearer. Over my shoulder I see a grey, pebbly beach and head for that, building up as much speed as I can to drive the boat up on to the stones. I lift the oars and grip the sides of the boat, bracing myself for the sudden jolt as the little boat hits the beach and scrapes to a halt. I breathe and take off my gloves. The cut that had almost healed is stinging and sore again; my hands are raw and trembling.

But I have done it. I am here.

22

As I clamber out of the boat, stiff and aching, I notice another groove in the snowy pebbles where a boat has been pulled up out of the water. Someone else has already been here this morning.

I look up at the grey folly – even more bizarre up close than it was from the water. Powdery snow has settled evenly on its ledges, sills and battlements, catching on the rough stone so that it looks as if it has been dusted with icing sugar – a witch's gingerbread house. Old Moll must be very strange indeed to live somewhere like this. The pathway to the door is guarded on both sides by a tangle of brambles. In fact, apart from the miniature castle, most of the island is either rock or bramble. There is no garden. The few trees that have managed to grow here are stunted and strange, twisted into weird shapes by the bitter wind.

I make my way up the path. Every footstep, every breath sounds ten times louder than it ever has before, and I am aware of my own heartbeat too. I put a hand on my chest and try to soothe it, as if it is a frightened animal.

The front door is made of thick oak, with big iron hinges and rivets – a child's drawing of a castle door. There is a knocker and I bang it once, twice.

'Forget summat, did yer mister?' a woman's voice calls – unexpectedly loud – as if she is just the other side of the door. I push, and it opens slowly, heavily.

There is no hallway, no passageway – the door opens into a single, large room with a stove at one end and a spiral staircase up into the turret at the other. The walls are bare stone, but hung with tapestries and swathes of brightly coloured velvet. A huge crystal chandelier hangs from the ceiling, blazing with light. The whole room is aflame with light and colour, but it is cold – freezing in fact. The stone floor is covered with Persian carpets and exotic animal skins; the dark furniture is draped with fabrics that even the late countess would have considered too showy; there are silver candlesticks, gold ornaments glowing in the light of a hundred candles . . . Everything is expensive, luxurious, but everything is covered in dust. Cobwebs blow in the cold draught.

There, in the middle of it all, is a sort of throne

upholstered in purple velvet, and sitting in the throne is a very large lady. Her dove-white hair is piled up on her head and fastened with jewelled hairpins. She is wearing a robe that flows over her enormous shape in cascades of purple satin.

Like a hermit, or a nun, Bryn had said. Not like any hermit or nun I've ever seen . . .

There is a silver cake-stand on a table next to the lady – it is laden with tiny cakes and Turkish delight and glittering crystallized fruits. She reaches out, takes a cake and pops it in her mouth. Gone. She chews and smiles in my direction.

After she swallows, she says, 'Got them papers for me t' sign already, mister?'

Of course – old Moll is blind. Her eyes are open and looking right at me, but they are cloudy-blue and dim.

'I – I'm not . . . mister anyone,' I struggle to explain. 'I'm someone else.'

Moll is silent for a moment. Then she says, 'Next t' no visitors in over ten year, and now two in one mornin'.'

'I'm sorry to disturb you, Miss Speedwell . . . I needed to see you.'

'Well, close th' door if you're comin' in, there's a breeze blowin' right up my legs.'

'Sorry. Yes,' I mumble. I push the door closed and walk a bit closer to her. 'I've come to warn you,' I say. 'The new earl, Clarence Asquith, is trying to get his hands on your money. He's going to send his solicitor . . .'

'Squeaky voice? Fetherington or summat?'

'Hetherington. Yes.'

'You just missed 'im.'

'You need to be careful, Miss Speedwell – Clarence will trick you and bully you. He'll take everything you have . . .'

'Everythin' I have?' she murmurs. Her sightless eyes move slowly around the room, as if they are taking in all the extraordinary trimmings of her life. How peculiar it must be, I think, to have all this luxury, but to be so utterly alone.

Moll finds a plate of chocolates on the table in front of her and holds it out. 'Truffle?'

'No, thank you.'

'They're from Belgium.'

'No, thank you. Did he try to make you sign anything – Mr Hetherington?'

'Said he'd help me keep me money safe. He's sortin' out all the paperwork to make sure it's officially mine. There should've been a contract, he said.'

'Well. It must be a ploy . . .' Either that or – is it possible he has decided not to help Clarence after all?

Moll eats another chocolate truffle. 'Who did you say you were?'

'I didn't.'

'Well?'

'I was hoping . . .' I realize a sob is rising in my throat and try to swallow it down quickly. 'I was hoping you might be able to tell me.'

Moll stares at me and, though I know she cannot see me, it is certainly as if she sees something.

'Come here, child,' she says, more gently.

I walk towards her, stepping carefully over the animal skins.

Moll indicates a dust-covered chaise longue, and I sit down.

'You think I delivered you?' she says.

'I don't know. But you might have.'

'If I did, I'll know,' Moll says. She holds her hands out towards me. They are small – almost like a child's hands. 'These hands will remember. Me eyes may've gone, and the rest of me's pretty useless now too, but these hands remember everythin'. Never lost a babby, not one, and it's all because of these small, clever hands. Come closer, child.'

I lean a little closer. She smells sweet – like sugared almonds.

Moll reaches towards me. I think perhaps she is going to feel the features of my face and I close my eyes tightly, but her hands move to my scalp instead. Slowly, gently, she feels the shape of my skull. It is a most peculiar sensation: soothing and strange – hypnotic. As she cradles my head, her small fingers working in circles over my skull, I start to feel almost sleepy. Then she stops.

She sits back in her chair. She takes a long, slow breath.

Then, very quietly: 'I thought you might come one day.'

'You know who I am?'

'O' course, child.'

'Tell me – please. Thomas Walters believes he is my father—'

'Aah, yes. Poor Thomas,' she says, shaking her head. 'Yes. You're his daughter right enough.'

A quick, cold breath rushes into me. *So, it is certain then.* My last, faint hope of a return to Gosswater Hall is blown away like dust. I take a deep breath. 'Then who is my mother?'

Moll smiles a very small, sad smile.

'Is she alive?'

'No, child. She's dead now. She died not long after you were born.'

I realize tears have spilt from my eyes and I wipe them roughly from my cheeks. 'Who was she?'

Old Moll sighs. 'Would you like a cake?' she says. 'Some Turkish delight? Crystallized ginger?'

'Who *was* she? What was her name?' I don't want to shout at Moll, I don't want to be rude, but this seems so cruel. *Why won't she just say?*

'I'm sorry, child,' Moll says at last. She brushes cake crumbs from her gown. 'I can't tell you. I wish I could

– I know what it must mean to you, but I can't. I promised I would never tell. An' it's a promise set in stone. Set in gold actually.' Her small, clever hands gesture to the luxury that surrounds us.

'If I tell you who you are, child, all o' this will be lost.'

23

At last – someone who can tell me the truth about who I really am, but the secret is still beyond reach: a casket, heavy with treasure, locked and dropped into the dark, deep water. Moll Speedwell would tell me nothing more. My frustration drives the oars back and forth, back and forth. I don't feel the tears freezing on my cheeks or the raw skin blistering on my palms; I don't feel the muscles burning in my arms and my back; I don't feel anything at all until I am back in Thomas's snow-deep garden, tying the little boat to the iron mooring ring. Then it all comes at once – a flood of pain and despair. I feel wounded inside and out.

I trudge up the length of the garden, placing my snow-heavy boots in the same bold footprints I made when I set out with such hope and determination just a few hours before. Back in the cottage, I light a fire and sit there staring into the flames. I don't know what happens next.

What happens next is lunch, says my brain. *You can't do anything on an empty stomach, Aggie.*

So I heat up Thomas's portion of the rabbit stew, and, as its rich warmth spreads through my body and limbs, I start to feel a little better.

I need something to do while my brain sifts through all that has happened. I fetch my needlework bag from my room. I always used to find needlework a calming thing to do – but my hand pulls out the sampler with the almost-finished Asquith family crest: IN AETERNUM FIDELIS, the motto reads. *Eternally faithful*. The only bit left to do is to embroider the roses that twine around the words, but I don't want to do that. Looking at the shield makes me think about the bequest in the earl's will – that I should be given a jewel that has been missing for my entire life. It strikes me now as a hollow gesture. Perhaps Clarence was right – perhaps the earl was mad after all. I shove the sampler back into the bag and decide to mend the threadbare cushion on Thomas's comfortable chair instead. I begin to stitch the shape of a goose over the worn patch. It will have Susan's face – accusatory, quizzical: an orange, black-tipped beak; beady blue eyes. I am surprised at how much it looks like Susan already. I think Thomas will like it.

The rhythm of stitching is soothing. The little fire crackles softly. It makes me think about what Bryn said: 'I'd give anything for a home like this.' It does feel like home now – more of a home than Gosswater Hall. *Would you go back, Aggie – if you could?* I try to remember what life as Lady Agatha felt like, but when I try to picture it in my mind, I don't see myself at all – I see Old Moll and her lonely life of luxury on Thorn Island. No: I don't think I would go back. But I don't seem to be able to go forward either. I am a clock stuck at midnight.

The rest of the afternoon passes slowly, sleepily, and so does the evening. Darkness creeps into the room, starting in the corners and spreading stealthily across the rug. I light a lamp. The snow starts to fall once more: Thomas will not be home tonight. I put more logs on the fire. I finish the cushion cover. I try to read *Hamlet*, but the words refuse to mean anything. I yawn for the hundredth time, and, eventually, I give in. The clock on the mantelpiece has been telling me it is bedtime for hours now. Its little painted moon looks at me reproachfully.

'All right, Moon,' I say. 'I'm going to bed now. I'll just check on the geese first.'

They usually rush at me as soon as I open the door, but the cold has got to them: they are tucked up, dormant. They hibernate together, huddling warmly in great downy clouds. I make sure they have plenty of food – grain, hay and vegetables. I find Susan and see that the King Stone is still safely hidden beneath her. She lets me look. She opens one pale-blue eye and looks straight at me. *I may have saved your life last night*, she seems to say, *but that does not make us friends.*

'Fair enough,' I say, and I feel moved to stroke the feathers on top of her hard, narrow head. 'Fair enough, Susan. Just keep the opal safe for me.'

She lets me stroke her for a moment, then she clacks her beak, closes her eyes again and tucks her head beneath her wing. Another goose settles close beside her. Suddenly, I can't bear the idea of going back into the dark, empty cottage all by myself; it feels wrong without Thomas there. Everything feels wrong. It is wrong that everything has been taken from me. It is wrong that I am entitled to nothing – not even to know who I am, who my mother is. So many unbearable wrongs . . . I button my coat right up to my chin, put my lantern safely on a ledge, and lie down in the clean straw. The geese huddle close, their warmth and softness surrounding me, keeping me safe. They can be soft and they can be fierce. Just like me. *It is possible to be more than one thing, Aggie* . . . I close my eyes. I won't stay here all night. But just for a while . . .

I am woken by the light – bright as a full moon. *I should close the curtains*, I think, but then I realize I am not in my bedroom – I am still here in the warm straw.

The geese babble and a shadow shifts. Someone else is here too.

I lie completely still, too terrified to move or lift my head. Cousin Clarence has come back for the King Stone. I will give it to him – I'm too broken to fight him, too tired.

Then a voice, soft as starlight – my name.

It is not Clarence. I lift my head and turn around. There is a goose sleeping beside me in the straw. It lifts its neck, raises its wings, and the white feathers take on a different shape altogether – the Ghost Girl. I hold my breath. I am still asleep – I must be. But the icy air is real, and so is the pain in my blistered palms as my nails curl into them.

She whispers her song – so softly, as if she is underwater, singing a mermaid lullaby. Her feather-white fingers reach out to touch my hair, and it is like being stroked by a moonbeam. I should be terrified, but I am not. *Who is she?* She is familiar – a little like me, a little like someone else. Her face is a soft, fierce blur of light.

She moves away then, towards the door. She beckons, and I follow her, spellbound, half-dreaming.

24

Sometimes she is a pearl-white lantern leading the way, sometimes she dances around me like thistledown. One moment she is there, the next she is a windborne snowflake or a fluttering moth of moonlight. The cold bites at my face, at my hands, but I barely notice it. I don't think about where we are going or why; my brain is peaceful, hypnotized – it trusts the Ghost Girl, as if it understands something I don't.

The lane ahead is a dark passageway beneath snow-laden trees, but she is a star, aflame with pure, white light. And here am I, pacing behind – mortal, booted, clad in black.

We move together through the night, twisting and turning until – quite suddenly – we are here, at the gates of Gosswater Hall. I could not have found it on my own. It is in darkness – no glaring lights as there were on New Year's Eve.

We follow the crescent of the driveway, to the bridge that crosses the moat. The Ghost Girl is fainter now, fading away. I go up the steps to the front terrace on my own, and push the door. It is not locked. It swings open at my touch. The atrium is dark as a cave. There is no fire burning in the hearth; a single candle flickers in its sconce at the foot of the stairs. I know where I must go. I walk silently up the carved staircase, my hand gliding over the familiar shapes and patterns of the old wood.

Just as I am thinking the Ghost Girl has disappeared completely, she is suddenly there ahead of me – bright as a gleaming chandelier. She is standing in front of the huge Asquith shield on the landing – a young woman in an ivory evening gown, dazzling, golden. *She belongs here – all this is hers.* She blazes like the sun, and then she is gone, and the darkness is even darker than it was before.

I keep walking, up to where she was standing just a moment before, then past the shield, and up the next flight of stairs. I walk past the guest bedrooms, past Clarence's room and Father's room. As I pass the door to my old bedroom, something jolts inside me: it is as if I have been sleepwalking and now I am suddenly, completely awake. What on earth am I doing here? I must be mad. What if Clarence is awake, and I meet him around the next corner?

But something is stronger than my fear – the echo of a song, a voice calling, crooning. I remember my final night here at Gosswater Hall – the night I stole the King Stone; I dreamt there was a voice calling me then . . . into the darkness of the Long Gallery. I feel a stab of fear in my chest. I have only dared to venture into the Long Gallery once. I saw a painting there in the gloom – a fox hunt – all blood and fur and twisted canine bodies. I turned and ran straight out again.

There is a dark gap in the curtains. I part them and creep through, ignoring the chill that shudders through my body. I try not to look at the pictures either side of me. *There is the fox hunt*, whispers my brain. *Here is a witch-burning, a sacrifice, a crucifixion . . .*

I keep walking, feeling smaller with every step. There is some kind of light ahead of me – a fine sliver of gold, and I know I must head towards it. I am passing portraits now – there must be hundreds of them – all those earls and countesses, lords and ladies who are entombed on Skelter Island. Their forbidding faces stare at me from either side. They hang here in the darkness, whispering of Asquith ancestry, Asquith history. They are here to tether us to the past; to tell us who we are. But not me. Not any more.

In front of me hangs a tapestry of geese attacking armed knights: the legend of the Queen Stone. The sliver of light is coming from behind it. I move the tapestry and it swings easily to the side. Behind it is a door, and it is open.

I step into a part of Gosswater Hall I have never been in before. Somewhere completely new.

It is a bedroom – a large, beautiful, brightly lit bedroom painted cornflower blue. The ceiling has been decorated to look like a summer sky: the same deep blue as the walls, but with the shapes of swifts and swallows soaring in flight and white clouds floating high above. I can almost feel the warm breeze on my skin. The smell of summer flowers and roses is as strong here as it was in the silvery tomb – stronger – and I know, without any doubt at all, that this is the Ghost Girl's room.

Or it was. Once.

It is in a dreadful mess – ransacked, just like the rooms of Thomas's cottage the other night. Jewellery boxes have been emptied on to the bed, a snowdrift of papers and letters lies on the carpet, pulled out of drawers. A large wardrobe stands open, with all the clothes – *beautiful clothes!* – yanked down from their hangers and strewn everywhere. I pick up one of the dresses. It is exquisite – the silk as soft as rainwater – the style is exactly the same as my own dresses . . . The cut too . . . Identical. I pick up another dress and another and another, and they are all alike – eerily familiar. A spidery shiver scuttles up my spine as I realize a horrible truth: all those years, the countess was dressing me up in someone else's clothes.

Who was she, the Ghost Girl? I rummage through the papers and letters until I find what I am looking for — her signature.

Rose

The ghost of the silvery tomb has a name at last. I remember the rose carved into the tree; I think of the inscription *Beloved*. She must indeed have been *beloved* — this room is like a shrine. Rose might have died yesterday . . . I start to feel uneasy. I notice a half-drunk glass of sherry on the dressing table, a half-nibbled sandwich. Every lamp in the room is lit and a fire is burning brightly in the grate — someone must have tended it recently, within the last hour. *What if they come back?*

I should go.

I put the silk dress and the letter back where I found them and tiptoe towards the door, but just as I reach out for the handle, I freeze. It is turning slowly from the other side.

25

'Agatha,' Clarence oozes, coming into the room. 'I had a feeling it might be you.' His face twists into a grimace. 'How nice of you to drop in.'

My heart is thundering. He looks monstrous, mad – he has purple circles around his eyes as if he hasn't slept in days. He's going to kill me. I know he is.

'Nowhere to run to now, little Agatha. No thug of a father to protect you, no vicious geese, and no sly little friend to help you hide away . . .'

He means Bryn. If only he were here with me, I wouldn't be so afraid.

I look instinctively at the door – my only way out. Someone will come, I think, breathing fast. If I scream, someone will hear the noise – a housemaid, an under-butler.

'Oh, and I've dismissed all the servants too,' Clarence says, as if he can read my thoughts. 'Sent them packing this afternoon – useless, untrustworthy, *disrespectful* bunch.'

I stare at him. *Dismissed all the servants?* He must be mad. The back of my neck prickles icy-cold.

'It's just you and me, Agatha. We can have a proper chat at last. Undisturbed. So, why don't you tell me what you're doing here, in *my* house in the middle of the night? Have you come to put the King Stone back where it belongs?' He tilts his head to one side, but it seems he is not expecting an answer. He saunters towards me. 'No. I didn't think so. You're looking for the greater prize now, aren't you? Just like me. Searching for the Queen Stone.'

'No, I . . .'

'Did you find it? Here in Rose's room?' His mouth is slack, but his eyes are burning feverishly. He steps even closer, slowly, slowly, then he seizes me by the shoulders: 'DID YOU FIND IT?'

'No! I didn't find it – I wasn't looking for it. I've never even been in this room before!'

He shakes me violently, as if he expects opals to jump from my pockets.

'Never been in this room, before! You're a terrible liar, Agatha.'

'I haven't!' I protest, struggling to get free from him. 'I was never allowed in the Long Gallery. I didn't know there was a hidden door . . .'

He studies my face and narrows his eyes. He is intrigued. 'You've never been in Rose's room before? Your own sister's room?'

A beat. *What?*

His eyes light up – he is a torturer finding a new, sharp little toy to play with.

'You know all about Rose, don't you – the earl and countess's first daughter? Or perhaps I should say their *real* daughter? They told you all about her, surely?'

His grip on my shoulders loosens at last, but I don't try to run. I can't move from the spot. I feel dizzy, weak. *Rose? Their real daughter?* And then another thought – strange and sad and beautiful all at once: *the Ghost Girl is my sister.*

'I never met dear Cousin Rose,' Clarence sniffs, 'my father chose to keep his distance from his brother, the late earl, but Odelia was able to fill me in on the details. Rose was adored by your parents. She was only eighteen when she died, and they were so devastated that they ended up taking you in, to fill the gap, as it were. But I imagine it's a bit like trying to replace a much-loved dog – even if you pick the same breed, it's always a disappointment.' He gives me a long, cruel look, and I look straight back, unflinching. 'People said the two things were connected – the loss of the opal and then, straight after, Rose's death: *the curse of the Queen Stone*, they called it – superstitious idiots. But if it's in the earl's will, then he must have known where it was – or at least he knew right at the end . . .' His eyes flick restlessly around the plundered room. 'I thought there was a sporting chance he had hidden the Queen Stone in here . . . But I can't FIND IT!' He suddenly spins around, sweeping a row of ornaments from the mantelpiece so they crash and shatter on the hearth tiles. 'I can't find it ANYWHERE in this damn house.'

I clench my fists. I won't let him see that I'm shaking. 'Why would the earl have *hidden* his own jewel, Clarence? That doesn't make sense.'

'I don't know, do I? The old fool was completely cuckoo. All I know is I *need* it.'

'You're forgetting that the earl left it to *me*.'

'BALDERDASH!' The mask of madness is upon his face once more – he lunges towards me, and his hands close around my throat, squeezing. 'The whole estate is mine; the Queen Stone is mine. I NEED it!'

'Even if he *did* tell me where it was,' I say hoarsely, writhing and clawing at his fleshy hands, 'I wouldn't tell *you*!' But then something happens in my head: *Perhaps he did tell you, Aggie*, my brain whispers. *Perhaps his final words meant something after all . . .*

Clarence sees the thought flash across my face.

'He *did* say something to you! What did he say?'

I can hardly breathe – everything is turning black. Clarence's face is a pinprick far away. Then he lets go of my throat. I gasp, the air rushing back into my lungs so fast it burns – my chest is on fire.

'Tell me what he said!'

I take a breath, rubbing my neck. I am thinking, buying time.

'TELL ME!'

'I'll tell you what the earl said if you let me see his will.' I want to see it. I am *sure* there are things in there that Clarence has been keeping from me . . .

'Ha!' An explosion of loud, manic laughter: 'You have nerve, Cousin Agatha, I'll give you that! Bargaining with me at a time like this, as if I couldn't despatch you as easily as that!' He snaps his fingers in my face, but I don't blink. 'I could throttle you; I could throw you out of the window,' he goes on, starting to enjoy himself. 'I could whistle for Brutus and let him do his worst, or make you run for your life across the estate with the whole pack of hounds after you . . .' He leans in close, his voice silky, 'No one would know or care that you had gone, would they, Agatha?'

Hatred and fear are scalding hot in my veins, but I manage to force a sweet smile. 'Do you want to know what the earl said or not?'

Clarence's mouth twitches, and he draws the will from his top pocket. 'I suppose I could let you have a little peek . . .' He holds it out, then jerks it back again, just out of reach. He raises his eyebrows: 'Well?'

'He said *Rose* just before he died. *Eternal Rose.* I didn't know he was talking about his daughter –

I thought maybe he meant . . .'

'What? Thought he meant—'

'Father loved the garden – I thought he was deliri-
ous – talking about a rose bush or something.'

Clarence looks towards the big arched window and
the dark gardens beyond – his eyes are alight with
greed once more. '*The eternal Rose* . . . You might be
right: *not* Rose's room, but a rose that flowers year
after year – life eternal! The Queen Stone must be in
the rose garden – buried treasure . . .'

I take my chance while he is distracted and snatch
Father's will from his hand.

'You little witch!' Clarence grabs the poker from
the fireplace, raising it above his head. I cringe away,
stumbling and crawling beyond its reach. I scramble to
my feet and run out of the room, through the shrouded
gloom of the Long Gallery, clutching the papers in my
fist. Clarence is yelling after me, but I don't stop and I
don't look back.

'There's no point running, you little thief!'
Clarence shouts. 'I'll call Brutus, I'll release the
hounds – I'll let them rip you to shreds! No one will
know if you die, Agatha, and no one will care . . .'

I am pelting down the corridor towards the main
staircase. I take the steps four at a time, flying around
the corner and down on to the landing. I slip on the
polished floor, my feet clumsy with fear. No one will
know if you die . . . and no one will care. No: Thomas

would know! Thomas would care! I skirt the final corner of the staircase. Then I hear Brutus barking — savage and terrible. I turn, panicked, lose my footing, and clutch for the bannister beneath my hand. For a fleeting, falling moment I see a familiar face in the carved pattern of the polished wood — its eyes meet mine. *Fox. Thomas's fox* . . .

The memory that has been evading me so successfully finally explodes in my brain, just as Gosswater Hall turns topsy-turvy, and I tumble down the stairs below.

26

I am lying at the foot of the stairs on the cold floor of the atrium. I can hear Brutus barking several floors above, and there are footsteps too – slowly pacing down the landing, the rhythmic drumming of a poker on the polished floor.

I take hold of the wooden pillar next to me and haul myself to my feet. My back and hips feel bruised, and my brain feels shaken in my skull. I take a second to steady myself. On the pillar, just by my hand, is the carving of a wren – bright-eyed and beak open, about to burst into song.

'Thomas,' I breathe. 'This is Thomas's work.'

But there is no time to think about that now. The deep, hostile barking is louder, closer – I picture Brutus galloping along the corridor towards the stairs, drool flying from his open jaws. I take a step towards the front door. My legs judder beneath me, but they still seem to work.

Bruised but not broken, my brain says. *Now let's go.*

I stumble and run down the driveway, slowing to a limp only once I am through the gates. The walk back to Thomas's cottage is long and dark and frightening. I rely on the faint glow of starlight on snow to find my way. The Ghost Girl is not here with me, but she is in my mind – adored daughter of the earl and countess; my long-lost sister: Rose. The winter wind gusts, scattering the clouds, and the moon appears for a moment, making the frozen road ahead gleam like a knife. I am nearly home. Once, twice, I turn back, convinced I can hear the distant barking of Brutus and the hounds. I walk faster, but my boot slides on the ice and I nearly fall. I can't tell if it is terror or the cold, but I start to shiver uncontrollably. I imagine the dogs tearing towards me through the darkness, teeth bared, paws flying, eyes blank with the chase. They have my scent and I am their quarry.

I think the shivering will stop when I am home and have locked the doors behind me, but it doesn't. It doesn't stop even when I put on my warmest clothes and sit beside the hot, crackling little fire in the parlour, cradling a cup of tea in my hands. I can still hear the baying of the hounds.

He'll come for you, my brain says, and I know it is not trying to frighten me; it is just trying to be practical. *You can't just wait here for Clarence to come and finish you off.*

But I have nowhere else to go and no one to turn to. Thomas is still not home — of course he isn't — the snow is deeper than ever. Until Ramskull Pass is clear, I will have to manage by myself.

I take the will out of my coat pocket and smooth it out on my lap with trembling fingers.

This is the last will and testament of Henry St John Asquith, Twenty-Ninth Earl of Gosswater and Lord of Gosswater Hall, Baron Brougham . . .

I move my eyes quickly over the paper, skipping the parts I don't understand, searching for my name . . .

The end is now near. For the purposes of legal clarity, justice and moral fairness I feel compelled to set things right. As is commonly known, dear Agatha is not our own child. Being female, illegitimate and unofficially adopted, I hereby acknowledge that she is ineligible to inherit any part of the Gosswater estate, which must, of course, in its entirety, be passed to the heir presumptive, my nephew, Clarence Mallory Asquith.

I crush the demon's name beneath my thumb . . .

Agatha may, of course, continue to live at Gosswater Hall until such time as she chooses to marry, or she may wish to live at the home of her real father, Thomas Walters of Goss Farm. The choice is hers.

But the choice wasn't mine. It was Clarence's! Anger seethes within me, never far from the surface: *Another thing he took from me . . .*

I turn the paper over. There is a lot about charitable donations that must be paid from the estate – including one to the orphanage in Penrith. That must be the orphanage the countess took Bryn to. The next thought brings a swift, light pain in my chest: that might be the orphanage where they found *me*.

My eyes are still scanning, my heart beating quickly and lightly. Here is my name mentioned for the last time – the part Clarence read to me before the fight with Thomas:

The Queen Stone is hereby bequeathed as a gift to Agatha. Although this is technically part of the Gosswater estate, I hope Clarence will choose to honour his uncle's last wish by allowing Agatha to keep this precious heirloom. I will tell her where to find it before it is too late. In addition to the Queen Stone, I would like Agatha to be given some of the countess's jewellery, so that she might have some small nest egg of her own. Again, legally speaking, this will be in the gift of the Thirtieth Earl. As executor, I also entrust Clarence Asquith to deliver the appended letter in which I seek forgiveness for the shameful secrets and wrongs of the past.

Not just the Queen Stone, but jewellery too – the earl wanted me to have a 'nest egg' of my own! But I know Clarence will never give these things to me freely. He will never give me anything. This must have been why he didn't want me to see the will – he was afraid I would make a claim on the opal and the jewellery. I swallow hard. He has every reason to want me out of his way. It would be very convenient for him if I mysteriously disappeared.

I read these parts of the will over and over. There is so much I don't understand. That phrase again: 'wrongs of the past' – forgiveness, justice, the truth . . . He talks about a private letter which should be attached but isn't. A letter to whom? And what does he mean by 'shameful secrets'? The part I keep coming back to is one of the simplest sentences in the whole document: 'As is commonly known, dear Agatha is not our own child.' In this one sentence, Father both disowns me and tells me that I am dear to him. I can't make sense of it. I cling to that word *dear*. In spite of everything – in spite of being a disappointment, a poor substitute, a shadow-daughter, acquired in an attempt to fill up the Rose-shaped hole in their lives – I was still dear to him. But he could never bring himself to show it.

The date next to the signature is *19th December 1899* – the day Mr Hetherington last called at the house. I look at the feeble scrawl of Father's initials – he must have been barely able to hold the pen. He clearly wanted to rewrite his will for a reason. He had had a change of heart about something important . . .

Then a different thought slides into my head.

Perhaps there *is* someone I can turn to for help . . . If I show the will to Bryn, it might help him to understand the whole sorry situation. Perhaps he will forgive me for not being more honest about who I really am.

The fire is dying now, and the sun will rise soon, but the hounds are still baying at the brink of my imagination. My body is still shivering. What I need is a friend.

27

By the time the rowing boat reaches Skelter Island, it is dawn. I sit there for a while, allowing my heart to slow itself as the water laps at the shore, gently dandling the boat. The sky has melted from black to silver, and I realize I can no longer hear the hounds.

Yes. This was the right thing to do.

I feel better for being closer to Bryn, for the steady rhythm of the rowing, and for putting a substantial stretch of water between me and Cousin Clarence. The snow-topped fells shimmer like rubies as the sun rises and light spills down into the valley. It feels like an eternity since I have seen daylight; I turn my face up to the eastern sky and drink it in.

I don't know yet what I will say to Bryn, or how I

will begin. So much has happened since our argument. I hope that he is not still angry with me – that he will give me a chance to explain . . . I am looking forward to seeing him so much that I half-expect him to be waiting for me here on the jetty, with a joke and a wry smile, but there is no sign of him. He is probably having his breakfast. My stomach rumbles at the thought of hot buttered toast. Perhaps I should go and find him.

There is a dirty, well-trodden path through the snow and I follow it all the way to the silent church. Here is the odd little shack he shares with Sexton Black, and smoke is snaking from the chimney, so someone must be up and about.

I lift my hand, but the door opens sharply before I have the chance to knock.

It is not Bryn; it is Sexton Black. I make myself as tall as possible.

'You,' he says. 'The girl from th' funeral. Th' Asquith girl.' He looks behind me as if he expects to see someone else too. There is something odd about him – he is strangely still. I realize that this is, perhaps, the first time I've seen him sober.

'Good morning, Sexton,' I say. 'I'm so sorry to trouble you at this hour. Is Bryn at home, please?'

'Bryn! That—' He sounds as if he is about to call him every wicked name under the sun, but then he stops himself. 'He in't with you?'

'Me? No.'

He gawps at me for a moment as if trying to work something out. 'Ah,' he says. Then, very slowly: 'He'll still be clearin' snow from th' footpaths, I'd think. Perhaps yer'd like to come in out o' th' cold and wait for him, little miss? Would yer like a cup o' tea?'

The thought of a steaming cup of tea is too good to resist. 'Thank you, sir.'

As he limps about, filling the kettle from a bucket and placing it on the rusty stove, I am struck by how different he seems from the drunken devil who chased us across the island on New Year's Eve.

'Yer come here in yer own boat, did yer, then?' he says, conversationally. 'Rowed across all by yer little self?'

'Yes. I'm getting quite good at rowing.'

He smiles at me – a weird, toothless grimace. 'Good for you, little miss.' Then he says, 'I'll just get a few more logs for th' stove. Make y'self comfortable. I'll be back in a jiffy.' And the rotten front door slams shut behind him.

I sit down and wait. The kettle bubbles and builds to a shrill whistle, and I use a foul-smelling cloth to lift it off the stove. I look around, but I can't see any cups anywhere, nor any tea, nor milk, and there isn't a hint of a piece of hot buttered toast. My stomach growls impatiently. I sit down and wait for a minute more. Where has Sexton Black got to? Surely the log store can't be that far from the shack . . . Then I notice something. There is a large pile of firewood stacked beside the stove – forty logs at least. The truth whispers through me.

He was lying.

I fling the door open and step out into the snow. I start to walk back down the slushy path, and I walk faster and faster until I am running at full pelt, the snow-dusted tombs and trees nothing but a grey-white blur as I race by. I don't know why I am running – I just know that something is very, very wrong. I see the sexton's eerie, toothless smile in my mind, and I am certain now that I have been tricked, but why? Tricked into what?

When I finally reach the water, it all becomes clear.

There, twenty yards or so from the shore, is my rowing boat, with the hunched figure of Sexton Black beating furiously at the water with the oars.

'HEY!' I shout, 'HEY! Come back! What are you doing?'

The sexton rests the oars and grimaces at me. 'Thank yer kindly for th' boat, little lady!'

'What? Wait! You can't take my boat!'

'I can and I 'ave! That sinful Bryn took my boat two nights ago and I 'aven't seen 'im since.'

Not seen Bryn for two nights? Then where . . .

'Run away, I'll wager – the ungrateful little worm. Took the boat an' left me here wi' no food, no booze, nothin'! When I catch him, I'll thrash him all the way t' HELL an' back.' He turns to face the fells behind him. 'Yer hear me? I'll THRASH yer, yer LITTLE WORRRRRM!'

The threat echoes from the rocks and quakes across the water. He takes up the oars again.

'Wait, Sexton – take me with you! You can't leave me here!'

'Don't tell me what I can and can't do, Miss High-an'-Mighty! Yer young squabs need t' be taught a lesson.' He starts to row. 'And *I* need to get t' the ale-house. Then I'll find that boy an' find me boat, get some more booze in . . . I might be back by nightfall, or mebbe tomorrow. Don't worry, little lady, yer won't be lonely – plenty o' ghosts t' keep yer company!' He throws his head back in a ghastly, gummy cackle.

'Sexton, *please!*'

But it is too late. He is thrashing through the water now, and there is nothing I can do but watch as the boat shrinks into the distance, its wake lapping at the pebbles beneath my boots.

28

I stand there for a minute, or perhaps it is an hour. After a while, the numbing cold drives me to move.

Come along, my brain says – its tone gentler than usual. *Let's get you warm.*

I make my way back to the sexton's shack and take a bitter pleasure in packing the old stove with as much firewood as I can possibly cram in. It burns like a furnace, and it isn't long before my knees and cheeks are scorching hot. I curl up on a chair, place my coat over myself like a blanket, and close my eyes.

When I open them again, it is almost dark. Have I slept all day? I must have. The church clock strikes the hour: four o'clock in the afternoon. I feel unbearably thirsty.

I drink a cup of boiled water from the kettle, then I rummage around in the larder. I find a stale biscuit and wolf it down in two bites. There is nothing else, just empty tins and jars. A thorough search of the shack reveals only a strange-smelling lotion for some sort of skin complaint and a tin of rat poison.

Rats. Bryn told me the island was covered with them. Could I catch one? And if I could catch one, could I bring myself to cook it and eat it?

No, my brain says, unequivocally. *No. You couldn't, Aggie. Someone will be here soon. Just hang on for a few more hours. At least you are warm. Things could be worse.*

Ha.

I think of Lady Agatha Asquith – the girl I used to be – so far away now she might as well be a character I once read about in a book. I think of her cinnamon crumpets for breakfast, her five-course lunches, her afternoon tea and cake on the terrace. And I think of the person who has stolen all this from me and turned me into a miserable, starving wretch who is actually considering eating a roasted rat. *Clarence Mallory Asquith, Thirtieth Earl of Gosswater* . . . Vengeance burns within me. The flames flare up, hotter than ever. I want Clarence to suffer as I am suffering now, and worse – much, much worse. He must be stopped, and he must be made to pay a price for what he has done to me. There is no way back to my old life now – I know that – but I have to do something with all this anger and hate and fear inside me. Perhaps revenge will bring me peace . . .

What on earth could I do, though, and how could I do it?

There are no answers written on the smoke-stained ceiling. My poor brain is hungry and exhausted. Eventually, I manage to soothe myself back to sleep by imagining what I know Clarence will be doing right now – digging up every single rose bed at Gosswater Hall on his wild goose chase for the Queen Stone.

The next time I wake up I feel oddly refreshed.

It must be the middle of the night now, or the early hours of the morning. The last embers of the fire are the only source of light; they glow red in the cold, black room. I wait and wait to hear the church clock strike, but there is only silence. Perhaps it needs to be wound every day, and there is no one here to wind it. No Sexton Black, and no Bryn.

Where can he be? He didn't come here after our argument, so where would he have gone instead? Is Sexton Black right – that he has run away from Gosswater for good? I think of the cruel blizzard that night. What if Bryn had some kind of accident in his boat?

I feel restless, and wide, wide awake. I light an oil lamp and put my coat on. As I step out of the door, I expect to be overwhelmed by the darkness and the presence of all those sinful ghosts, but it is oddly peaceful. The light of my lantern only reaches a few feet, so I feel as if I am walking in a bubble of light, floating through utter darkness. I wonder if this is what it feels like to be the Ghost Girl.

I crunch through the snow to her silver-grey tomb, thinking of that shadowy, shivery night when Bryn and I hid from Sexton Black in here. Snow has stuck slightly to the marble, and I brush the icy crust away to reveal the word BELOVED. And then, as if guided by an invisible hand, I lift the tangled fringe of ivy that hangs above the inscription. There, hidden beneath it, is the name of my sister:

ROSALIND VICTORIA ASQUITH

A thought shuffles quietly into my mind: Father's last words to me – the hiding place of the Queen Stone. Could Rose's tomb be the 'eternal rose' he spoke of? Oh – and there is the rose cut into the silver birch too! I hold my lantern up and examine the flower gouged into the tree; I touch the carved petals and thorns with a gloved finger. Did the earl put this here as a marker or clue?

At the door of the tomb I draw back the thick bolt, and step inside.

It feels empty. The flickering light of my lantern reveals four grey walls, a low ceiling, and a stone coffin on a stone table. If there *is* anything hidden in here, it could only be inside the coffin. I don't consider myself squeamish – not any more – but I'm not about to crack open a coffin on my own in the middle of the night.

Rose isn't in there, whispers my brain. *Her spirit has flown. It's just old bones.* I picture a skeleton in a silk dress and shudder horribly, as if I've glimpsed my own inevitable fate.

I touch the cold edge of the box, feeling that I ought to say a prayer or something.

'I wish I had known you, Rose,' I say instead, realizing how much I mean the words only once they have been spoken. I think of the stark solitude of my childhood and – just for a moment – I allow myself to imagine what it might have been like to grow up at Gosswater Hall with a sister by my side, with parents who weren't so consumed by grief that they could barely see me. The only light in the tomb comes from my lantern, but the smell of roses is suddenly all around me – sweet as a midsummer evening.

Clarence was convinced the 'eternal rose' was a clue to finding buried treasure, but I am certain that there is no treasure to be found here in this tomb. I look at the coffin one last time before I leave, and then bolt the door behind me. Father would never have hidden anything here. He wouldn't have disturbed his daughter's resting place.

I jump slightly when my brain pipes up, its voice particularly impish: *Clarence doesn't know that, though.*

What?

Clarence doesn't know this tomb is empty. And there's the 'eternal rose' carved on the tree outside ... He's so desperate to find the Queen Stone, if you told him it was hidden here, he'd fall for it like a hawk to a glove.

And then what?

And then ... My brain whispers the most insidious, brilliant plan. One simple trick that will bring me all the things I want in one fell swoop. If I get it right, it will deliver the truth into my hands; it will protect me from Clarence for ever; it will allow me to bury all that seething anger and hatred once and for all. It will be the ultimate act of justice and vengeance.

29

Back in the stinking shack, I spend the remaining hours of the night plotting. Black thoughts swirl around my head like smoke. By the time the sun rises, I know exactly what I am going to do to Clarence and how I will do it. I am almost vibrating with anticipation. Now all I have to do is get off this wretched island.

I walk all around its shoreline, hoping that I might stumble across a forgotten vessel of some kind, or a handy pile of materials to construct my own raft, but there is only snow and rock, dead leaves and the storm-wrecked nests of waterbirds. I search the lake for any sign of a boat, but the water is as still as glass. More snow has fallen in the night and the temperature must have dropped further; the ice around the reeds and rocks seems to be creeping further and further into the body of the lake. I am just about to give up and head back to the shack for another cup of hot water when something catches my attention in the distance – the flap of a large, white wing. A swan? A heron?

No . . .

I sit very still and squint at the shape as it gets closer.

My heart is excited, and so is my empty stomach. *A boat – it's a sailing boat!*

Now I am torn – do I stay here and wave and shout? Do I go and fetch dry wood from the shack to build a signal fire?

I decide to stay put and shout – I can't risk dashing back to the shack, missing my chance and the boat just sailing by.

The skiff tacks this way and that, slowly zig-zagging across the water, its white sail flapping to catch each flurry of winter wind.

I take off my warm coat, run a branch through its arms and turn it into a black sail of my own. When the boat is next tacking towards me, I wave the huge flag to and fro above my head, yelling at the top of my lungs: 'HEY! OVER HERE! HELP! HEY!'

The boat tacks away again, and I am certain I have not been seen, but when it turns back, its course is directly towards me.

I can see a figure now – a tall, broad figure dressed in red.

It is a young woman.

'Hullo!' she calls as the hull of the skiff grounds on the narrow, pebbled beach. 'Do you need rescuing?'

'Yes! Yes – thank goodness! Thank you for stopping.' I dismantle my flag and put my coat back on. I have ripped the silk lining of the left sleeve but I don't care in the slightest.

She leans towards me and puts out a hand to help me get in. I launch myself at the skiff and the woman hauls me over the side. I land with a bump in the bottom of the boat, winded and startled. She laughs, and I am surprised to find myself laughing too.

'Well, now I know what a fish feels like when it's been caught,' I say, and she laughs again.

Above me, the woman's face is upside down – an open-mouthed smile, a wave of long black hair. Despite the folds of her warm red cloak, I can make out the rounded shape of her stomach: she is expecting a baby.

'Are you all right?' she asks.

I nod and rub my hip – already black and blue from my tumble down the stairs at Gosswater Hall.

'Fine – just a bit bruised.' I manage to untangle myself and sit up on a low bench at the edge of the boat. 'I'm Aggie.'

'Ivy.' She grins, shaking my hand firmly.

I smile back. 'Ivy the baker's daughter? Old Moll's niece?' Bryn mentioned her – sailing her skiff up the lake to take supplies to Thorn Island.

She nods and laughs again. 'Aye, Ivy Speedwell – Moll's *great*-niece. Pleased to meet you. I'm on my way back home now if you'd like a lift to the village? Or can I drop you somewhere on the way?' As she talks, she jumps out of the boat, leans against the stern and pushes it off the pebbles, splashing through the knee-deep icy water before climbing back in again.

'Would it be possible to drop me over there?' I point to the opposite side of the lake, towards Thomas's cottage. Ivy thinks about it, checking the wind, glancing up at the heavy black sky.

'I could,' she says at last. 'But it'll take us a long time with the wind gusting against us, and I think there's more snow on its way. It'll be quicker and safer to go straight back to the village, I think. You can catch a lift home on a cart. Will that be all right?'

I nod. Anything is better than another day alone on Skelter Island.

'How'd you get marooned, Aggie?' Ivy asks. 'A ship-wreck? A mutiny?' She is smiling whilst doing something complicated with the ropes attached to the sail. 'Hold on!' she calls as the sail fills and we tip suddenly to one side. I clutch hold of the edge of the boat, alarmed. But then we start to gather speed and the boat soars over the water. Ivy leans back, closes her eyes and smiles broadly. I close my eyes too and enjoy the rush of cold air on my face, the smell of the spray. It feels like I am the wind itself. It feels like freedom.

When I open my eyes again, Ivy is smiling straight at me. 'It's like nothing else on earth,' she says. 'Like flying.'

I smile back.

'Well?' she says. 'How *did* you get stuck on the island?'

I consider a few different versions of the truth and end up choosing the one that is simplest and most plausible. 'I went there to visit my friend Bryn, but he wasn't there, and Sexton Black stole my boat so he could go to the village.'

She sniffs. 'Sexton Black. He's a nasty piece of work.'

I nod wholeheartedly.

'You'll need to duck down in a moment, Aggie,' Ivy says. 'I've got to swing the boom across.'

I crouch down into the hull and when I dare to pop up again, the village shoreline is looming ahead. Next to me in the bottom of the boat there is an empty box labelled *Chocolats Belges*.

'Have you been to see Old Moll this morning?' I ask. 'Have you taken her some food?'

'Aye,' Ivy says. 'I wanted to get there and back before the weather closed in.' She laughs. 'Strange old bird is our Moll. What a way to live!'

'I went to see her – a couple of days ago.'

'Really?' Ivy is surprised. 'Old Moll doesn't see

anyone. Hasn't seen the rest of the family in over ten years.'

'I didn't give her much choice. I just turned up. I wanted to ask her about my mother – she delivered me, you see, when I was born.'

'Old Moll delivered most people round here.' Ivy smiles, but she is concentrating on getting the boat safely to its mooring now.

'She knows who my mother is, but she won't tell me. Something to do with being afraid of losing all her riches.' I don't know why I am telling Ivy all this. Perhaps I am hoping that she might be able to persuade her great-aunt to change her mind . . .

Ivy tuts absently, as she turns and slows the boat. 'A curse, if you ask me, those riches. Driven a wedge into our family. My dad hates me taking food up to her – says she can rot for all he cares. Silly old crone says she's worked hard all her life and she's determined to end her days like a queen. Well, who wants to be a lonely, fat queen, I ask you? She won't listen to reason. Here – hold this.'

Suddenly, Ivy is moving everywhere at once and I have to hold a rope while she sorts out the sail. She steps out on to the jetty and I have to throw her a different rope whilst holding tight to the first one. It is all a bit of a blur. Before I know it, we are both standing on the jetty, the boat bobbing obediently beside us, and she's shaking my hand again. 'A pleasure to meet you, Aggie.

Will you be all right now? I can help you find a lift home if you like.'

'I'm all right,' I say. I have decided to crack on with my plan and walk straight to Gosswater Hall. What I need to do won't take long, I hope. And from there, I know I can find my way home to Thomas's cottage. 'Thank you for your help, Ivy.'

'You're sure you're all right? You look a bit pale.'

'I'm fine. I just – I haven't had any breakfast yet.'

'Here – take this.' She holds out a basket. 'Old Moll always orders far too much – and she told me to take this away. I'd hate for it to go to waste . . .'

I look in the bag and see a whole cherry cake and another box of the *Chocolats Belges*.

'Thank you, Ivy,' I say. I don't know if I have ever been so grateful for anything in my entire life.

30

I don't know Gosswater village very well – I have only been here a few times. The high street is quiet – a few people with their parcels of shopping, wrapped up against the cold; a couple of pony carts sloshing through the muddy snow. After I have devoured a few fistfuls of cherry cake, I make my way past the shops, looking for a road that will take me out of the village, up the hill, past the King's Head, where the Boxing Day hunt met, and then around the eastern shore of the lake to Gosswater Hall. I am – for once – looking forward to seeing Clarence, and baiting the trap . . .

I take a steep, icy road that goes past a seedy ale-house called the Swan Inn. I gawp through the windows as I walk by, looking for Sexton Black, but if he *is* in there, I can't see him through the smoky fug. There was no sign of my rowing boat at the jetty either. Perhaps the sexton has had his fill of liquor and has gone back to the island. Or perhaps he is searching for Bryn.

As I trudge through the slushy streets, I allow myself to start worrying about poor Bryn again. Where could he have gone? I remember the conversation we had by the fireside: he said he was afraid to go back to Skelter Island. Could he have rowed to the village instead? In that blizzard? Does he have any friends here he might be staying with? I curse myself for not thinking to ask Ivy if she'd seen him.

I am out of the village now and the snow lies thicker on the road here. I pass the King's Head, then a farmhouse and a few labourers' cottages, but I see no one at all. They must all be snug by their firesides. What fool would be out walking in weather like this? A large black bird lands on a low branch in front of me, and I salute it quickly – an old habit. Asquiths don't salute magpies, like normal folk – they salute ravens. Ravens have nested on the roof of Gosswater Hall for centuries, and there is a silly superstition that if they should choose to leave, the roof will fall, and so will the Asquith family. So I was always told to salute ravens politely and say, 'Fly on home now, sir.' But, as I look into this fellow's beetle-black eyes, I decide that I will not say the words. The Asquith line now ends with Cousin Clarence after all . . . The raven ruffles his big black wings; his sharp beak gleams like a sabre. He stays where he is, and I keep walking.

After another steep climb, I come to a crossroads. There is no signpost. I look around, trying to get my bearings, but I can't see the village or the lake from here at all – the world is just a white haze of snow-fleeced fields and grey stone walls. I stare hopelessly at the three different roads in front of me, wishing I had paid more attention when we drove to and from the King's Head on Boxing Day. A stream trickles noisily down the side of the track to my right, spilling between frosted rocks and stiff, frozen grasses. It then runs beneath the road through a clay gutter and out again on the left of the track. I dismiss this route: it must head downhill back to the lake.

Straight on, or right, then?

I have a vague sense that I need to be higher – to climb over this hill before dipping back down to Goss-water Hall.

I take the track to my right, following the stream uphill.

I walk and walk, stopping occasionally to scoop up a handful of ice-cold water from the stream. I eat another chunk of cherry cake. I am tired out, but somehow I keep trudging onwards. It occurs to me that I have no idea how long this journey should take on foot. Twice as long as a carriage ride? Three times as long? I must be nearly there, then. Unless – is it possible that I have somehow missed the turning? Should I go back?

The days are short at this time of the year. I am warm from walking, but a cold ripple of fear washes over me as I realize the light is fading already. The clouds above are black and heavy.

Come on, Aggie – keep going. You don't want to be stuck out on these fells at night in a blizzard.

After another half hour it is getting harder to make out the road ahead. Darkness is claiming the further distances and the quiet light is ominous. The road is narrow here, twisting and turning uphill like a sheep track. The snow is deep and undisturbed. My boots kick their way through it – exhausted, determined. I am trying to ignore the anxious mutterings of my brain: *It's getting dark. You're too high now. This doesn't feel right.*

There is something beside the road ahead. A signpost? I wade towards it through a deep snowdrift, stumbling, shoving snow away with my hands as if I am swimming. *Please let it be a signpost.*

The shape of the thing on top of the post is unmistakable.

It is not a sign.

It is a skull.

Two round, empty eye sockets stare down at me. The jawbone is long and slender, and it has curling, pointed horns. If I didn't know what it was, looming above me like a monster in the dreadful twilight, I would think it was the devil himself.

Well. You know where you are now, don't you, Aggie?

Yes, I do. It may not be a signpost, but it is as good as one. I am at Ramskull Pass. Somehow, I have trekked all the way up to the top of the fells. Thomas's cottage and Gosswater Hall are far below me. I turn around. I can see nothing but anonymous fields, the road a pale thread twisting down into the blur below.

You should have gone straight on.

Yes. But there's no time for recriminations now; the snow is starting to fall. Huge flakes are tumbling down like tufts of wool. It's too late to turn back – and the steep track downhill will be far too dangerous in the darkness and the snow – I'll slip and fall and freeze to death. I look around again, praying that as night falls I'll see a lamplit window or the distant flicker of a fire somewhere, but there is nothing at all.

Wait.

There *is* something. Not a light, but a structure of some kind – an abandoned cottage, perhaps – in the field to my right. It's far off – tucked in close against the white hillside. I blink at the snow, and make a visor of my gloved hand. I can definitely make out a wall, a low roof. It might be my only hope.

I clamber over the stone wall and jump down. The snow is shallower on this side and my knees jar painfully as I land. I turn back and salute the ram's skull, just as I did the raven; I'm going to need all the luck I can get to survive a night up here.

There are a few sheep tracks through the snow, but most of them head downhill. That's where all the sheep will be now – on the lower, more protected slopes.

Because they are cleverer than you, Aggie, my brain mutters unhelpfully.

One of the tracks, however, does not lead downhill: it leads to exactly where I want to go – the abandoned cottage.

A hundred yards closer, and it appears to be more of a shack than a cottage.

A hundred more, and I wonder if it is even that. It looks more like a pile of stones.

Another fifty and the truth becomes clear: it is not, in fact, a human habitation. It is just a sheep shelter. No hearth for a fire, not even a door to close against the wind: it is little more than a sheep-pen with a roof, to protect animals stranded up here in the harshest weather.

Well, that's what you are, after all, Aggie – just a stranded animal.

But there must be another stranded animal making use of the shelter too – the tracks I'm following lead straight into the low, dark, tunnel-like entrance. I crouch down on all fours and peer in, balking at the smell of dung, urine, wool-grease.

It is pitch-black in there.

I try not to think about the nature of the soft sludge I am crawling through.

A noise.

I stop.

Something is moving. It must be the sheep that made the tracks. It sounds frightened. I can hear it breathing – just a few feet away from me.

It's definitely a sheep – isn't it?

Of course it's a sheep. What else could it be, Aggie? A bear? A wolf?

What if it *is* a bear or a wolf? How quickly could I crawl backwards out of the tunnel if something were to fly at me? Not quickly enough.

It's just a sheep, Aggie – of course it's a sheep. It's frightened because it's stupid and it thinks you *are probably a bear or a wolf.*

'Shhh, now,' I say out loud, my voice trembling. I try to copy the soft tone Thomas uses for the pony when he's spooked. 'Ea-sy. Shhh, now. It's all right. I won't hurt you . . .'

And then the sheep answers me.

'Aggie? Is that you?'

31

'Bryn?'

My hands reach out in the darkness, and meet his fingers – cold as icicles. 'Bryn? What on earth . . . ? Are you all right?'

'Aggie . . .' His voice is very quiet.

I feel his arms, the deathly chill of his skin beneath his thin clothes.

I shuffle around so that I am sitting next to him and I put my coat over us both. I take his hands in mine and rub them, then I put my warm gloves on him, and my hat. 'Bryn?'

Nothing.

I rummage in the bag Ivy gave me, find the box of chocolates and tear it open. I fumble one into his mouth. 'Eat this, Bryn.'

After a moment, I hear him chewing and swallowing. 'Mmmm,' he breathes, almost inaudibly.

I give him another chocolate, and then another. I shuffle even closer and think I can feel a warmth spreading through his body at last.

It is a while before he has the strength to talk.

'Am I dreamin'?'

'I don't think so, Bryn. I think we're both really here, at Ramskull Pass in the middle of a snowstorm, sitting in a pile of sheep dung.'

He is smiling – I think.

'I were trying t' get to Penrith,' he says.

'How long have you been here? Since . . . that night?'

He shakes his head. 'I couldn't go back t' the island, so I rowed t' the village. I slept in the stables o' the Swan Inn – they were goin' to give me a job there, but then Sexton Black turned up – askin' folks if they'd seen me.'

'What did you do?'

'I ran. Set off across the fields so he couldn't follow, and then decided I might as well keep goin' all the way over the fells t' town – he'll not find me there. But I fell in a rabbit hole covered wi' snow and twisted my blasted ankle. I managed to crawl into this shelter and . . .'

'And then I came.'

'Well – you took your time about it, but, yes. A

night and a day later, Lady Agatha Asquith of all people comes t' my rescue.'

I feel my cheeks flushing in the darkness.

'That's not me any more, Bryn. I'm just plain Aggie now.'

I explain the whole sorry story to him. Father's death, Cousin Clarence, the discovery that I am not an Asquith after all. Then I tell him about the King Stone and the Queen Stone, about Father's will, and a missing letter that tells of a shameful secret. Finally, I tell him about my adventures since he left, getting stranded on Skelter Island and how I got lost on the way to Gosswater Hall, ending up here.

'By!' he murmurs, stunned.

'I'm sorry I let you think I was someone else, Bryn.'

He is quiet for a moment, letting it all sink in. 'I were thinkin' about it all as I was sittin' here, freezin' to death, and I decided that bein' angry with you for being a toff weren't fairly right. And it weren't fairly right o' me to hold a grudge about the countess puttin' me in the orphanage either. She thought she were doin' a good thing, didn't she?'

'I'm sure she did.'

'Hah – if she'd adopted me too, we might've been brother and sister, me an' you.'

'That wouldn't have been so bad, Bryn,' I smile.

'Aye,' he says quietly. Then: 'I made a promise to myself, sittin' here. If I come out of this scrape alive,

I'm going to be better. Let go of everythin' that's happened up to now. I decided I am goin' to have a shinin' future, and you can't have one o' those if you're draggin' a ton of muck about wi' you.'

We were both at a sort of crossroads last night, I think. *And we chose very different paths* . . . Bryn might be able to let go of everything that's passed, but I know that is impossible for me. My future *will* be shining eventually, but there is a battle to be fought first: a quest for the truth; a monster to be slayed . . .

'Any road, I'm sorry for shoutin' at you like that, Aggie. You can't help what you're born to, any more than anyone else.'

'That's just it, though, Bryn – I still don't know exactly what I was born to. Thomas is my father, but he hasn't told me anything about my mother at all, or how I ended up with the Asquiths. He was close to telling me, I think, but then he went to Penrith and he hasn't been able to get back because of the snow. Old Moll Speedwell can't or won't tell me anything. It's like the past is all bundled up and squirrelled away. I don't know who I am, Bryn.'

'Ah,' he says. 'Now that's a different thing entirely, m'lady. The past can tell you where you've come from, right enough, but it can't tell you who you are. Who you are is up to you right now.'

I think about this for a moment. 'How did you get to be so wise, Bryn Black?' I ask.

'It's amazin' the things that come t' you when you're sittin' in a pile of frozen sheep dung, waitin' for the Grim Reaper t' harvest your mortal soul.'

I smile. I've missed him.

'But the Queen Stone is yours, Aggie – the white opal – the old earl said so? An' jewels too?'

'Yes. Well, legally they belong to Clarence, but the earl wanted me to have them. He wasn't allowed to split the estate, you see.' I shake my head. 'Heaven knows where the white opal is, though – it's always just been a myth to me. Clarence is convinced it has been hidden somewhere and he's desperate to find it. He thinks he can't be a real Earl of Gosswater without it . . .'

'And the King Stone?' Bryn says.

'Well, I'm sure he'd like that back too – it's very valuable. He called it the "talisman" of his reign.'

A pause.

'Is it still underneath that goose?'

I laugh. I can't help it. Laughter bubbles up from somewhere deep inside me: 'Yes – it's still underneath that goose . . .'

Bryn is laughing too now, and the laughter takes over all of me until I am silently shaking and my tummy hurts, and I can feel Bryn shaking beside me too, and this makes me laugh even more, and there are tears running down my face.

It takes a good few minutes for the laughter to ease,

but when it finally does I feel warm all the way through, and achy and incredibly tired. I yawn a huge yawn. 'Oh, Lord, what are we going to do, Bryn?'

'I don't rightly know,' he murmurs sleepily, his head resting on my shoulder. 'We'll work it all out in the mornin'.'

'Yes. In the morning . . .'

'Aggie?'

'Yes?'

'Can I have one more o' them chocolates, please?'

32

I am woken by the thin, cold light that struggles towards us through the stone tunnel, and by the ache in my legs, my back and neck. I groan, and Bryn groans too – in real pain.

'Let's have a look at that ankle, then.'

Even in the feeble light, I can see that it is very swollen. Bryn flinches and gasps as I touch it.

'We can't just sit here until it heals, though, Bryn.'

'I'll manage,' he says. 'Ho-way, lass. We'll go down t' Penrith. I know a lad apprenticed to a blacksmith there – he'll help me find work and somewhere to stay, and you can find Thomas and come back home wi' him when the pass is clear.'

I don't say anything at all for a few moments. I can't say what I am thinking – that I am itching to go back home to find Clarence so that I can put my plan into action. But Thomas will be there in Penrith, and I can't let Bryn make the journey alone . . .

The better part of me wins: 'Yes. We'll go on to Penrith,' I say. *After all*, my brain mutters to itself, *revenge is a dish best served cold.*

I help Bryn out of the sheep shelter, pulling him through the slime of the tunnel. Then we find a sturdy stick for him to use as a crutch, and he leans on my shoulder for support. When we get to the road, I show Bryn the ram's skull, but it seems the two of them have already met.

They study each other in silence. 'I heard it the first night I were there in the shelter,' Bryn says in a voice that is quieter than usual. 'A high, ghostly bleatin' – fearsome it was, all night long. Like folks say: *Beware! Beware!* It got louder and louder. That's when I thought death were comin' for me.'

'It might have been an owl,' I say, but neither of us believes me.

Bryn turns his face to the wind. 'It's changed,' he says, closing his eyes. The wind ruffles his red hair. 'It's southerly now. You can feel the warmth in it.'

It doesn't feel particularly warm to me, but it's a bright enough day and it isn't snowing any more – which is something.

The road is easier than the fields – icier, but more even, and we start to limp along, gathering a bit of momentum as we find a comfortable rhythm.

At Ramskull Pass, the wind lifts the drifted snow and blows it across us in flying white waves – but as we go further down the valley, it becomes a gentle breeze, and I can feel that it really is warmer, as Bryn said. The streams are flowing beneath the ice, running through the snow-laden rocks and heather like sparkling roots.

'Talk to me, Aggie,' Bryn says, wincing. He wants me to distract him from the pain.

I tell him the part of the story I missed out last night. I tell him about Rose – how she was the earl and countess's first daughter – their real daughter – and that it was her tomb we hid in together on New Year's Eve.

Bryn listens quietly, and then says, 'You did see summat that night, didn't you?'

I keep walking, looking down at the snow and slush. At last I find the right words to tell him about the Ghost Girl. It is easier because we are walking side by side, and he isn't looking at me directly. If Bryn hadn't confessed to hearing the ghostly bleating of the ram's skull, I don't think I'd have ever told him. *This is what friendship feels like*, I think: a leap of fear and faith, trusting that your words will be understood.

Bryn keeps hobbling, concentrating hard on not slipping. Then he says, 'What d'you think she wants – the ghost?'

I have given this a great deal of thought. 'Do you

remember what Sexton Black said about ghosts coming back to right the wrongs of the past?'

'Aye. And it were in that chant we made up too. D'you think it's that?'

I nod. 'It's a bit like in *Hamlet*.'

'Hamlet? Isn't that the little village on t'other side of Gosswater?'

'No – yes, that is *a* hamlet, but not *this* one. *Hamlet* is a play by William Shakespeare.'

'Who?'

'It doesn't matter. It's a story – about a prince who is visited by the ghost of his dead father, who tells him that he was murdered.'

'Murdered?'

'Yes. Murdered by his own brother, the prince's uncle.'

'An' this is a play? It sounds brilliant. D' you think they'd ever show it at the playhouse in town?'

'I expect so, Bryn. The point is, the ghost wants Prince Hamlet to avenge his death: to kill his murderous uncle.' For a brief, delicious moment, I imagine running Clarence through with a rapier, then I close my eyes and shake the thought from my mind. It slinks off reluctantly, like a rat shooed away from a carcass.

'But Hamlet just isn't that sort of prince,' I say.

Bryn stops. 'An' what about you, Aggie? Are you that sort o' prince?'

I stop too. For a long, cold moment I am afraid that

Bryn has seen right through me — that he can see my plan for vengeance written on my face. Perhaps I even mumbled something out loud in my sleep.

He laughs. 'I'm jokin', Aggie.'

I manage to laugh too. 'Anyway, Hamlet can't really get to grips with revenge. What he really wants is justice, and the *truth*. And I think that's what the Ghost Girl wants too: she wants me to discover the truth.'

'Well, you have, haven't you? Perhaps Rose will rest peacefully now you know who she is. Who she *was*.'

I nod. 'Yes.'

But there are secrets buried deeper, Aggie, my brain whispers, and my fingers twitch impatiently. There is still some digging to be done . . .

33

The further down the fell we go, the wetter the snow becomes; the icy little waterfalls are necklaces dripping with diamonds in the morning sunshine. We stop frequently to drink from them and so that Bryn can rest.

'Any more scran?' he says with a grin, as if Ivy's bag might produce more chocolate or cherry cake all by itself, like the never-ending porridge pot, but he knows we finished the last of the food hours ago.

I try not to say, 'How much further?' too often, and he tries not to moan about his ankle.

We see more sheep on this side of the fells, and – at last – some farm buildings. I feel the most enormous sense of relief. *Civilization!*

The lower we get, the easier the road becomes. It is

clear enough for carts and carriages here, and we both get stupidly excited when Bryn spots a pile of fresh, steaming horse dung.

A few minutes later, a farmer passes us, and then stops. Before long our dreadful ordeal is over: we clamber into the back of the cart and are jolted and jiggled along, all the way to Penrith.

The farmer drops us off just outside the church.

'Thank you!' Bryn calls again, waving as the cart splashes around the corner. He holds out his hand to me.

'What?'

'We need t' say goodbye, I think, Aggie.'

I don't want to say goodbye, but I shake his outstretched hand.

'I need to fill up my bait bag –' he pats his stomach – 'an' find my blacksmith pal, and you need to go in there. This is the church Thomas is workin' in, in't it?'

I turn to look. The church is handsome, huge and square, the long nave twice as tall as it should be, so that it resembles the wing of a mansion.

'Yes. This is the one.'

The earl and countess were married here a long, long time ago. And this is where we always came for Easter and Harvest Festival, and Christmas too when the pass was clear. Mother preferred it to the humble little church in Gosswater village, or the church of the plague-dead on Skelter Island. As a child, I liked to look at the Giant's Grave – a huge burial plot marked by towering tombstones over ten feet tall. Miss McCarthy would take me out of the family pew when I got too restless during the service. She would hold my little gloved hand and allow me to babble away, making up stories about the giant who was buried here.

I take Bryn's hand again. 'Look at this,' I say, and pull him over the mound of snowy grass.

'By!' he exclaims, as he takes in the length and breadth of the grave. 'He must've been a big lad!'

'I think historians say it's probably a mass grave – like a vault – for an entire family, but it's much more fun to think there's a real giant buried here, isn't it?'

Bryn grins and nods. 'Let's just hope *he* doesn't rise from the dead.'

We both gaze down at the grave. The dark thoughts swirl again, and I imagine a great, fearsome warrior, twenty feet tall – a Goliath – striding down the driveway of Gosswater Hall towards a cowering Clarence . . .

'Aggie?'

'Yes?'

Bryn is giving me a hard stare.

'You're not goin' to do anythin', are you – when you go back?'

I keep my eyes fixed on the grave. 'What do you mean?'

'I just had a funny feelin', when you were talkin' about that play, and revenge and everythin' . . . You aren't goin' to do anythin' . . . stupid?'

'Stupid?'

'Promise me you'll just keep out of the way of that cousin o' yours. I can see what a mess it's all been, and what a rough shock, too, but – well, you've got a new home, and you've got Thomas Walters. A lot of people would be glad of a father like 'im. Let your cousin keep his riches. Forget about Gosswater Hall and Lady Agatha, an' try to be happy just bein' Aggie, won't you?'

'It's not about riches any more,' I say quietly.

'Well, stop poking at the past, then. What's gone is gone. And let Clarence alone. He's the sort who'll come to a sticky end in his own good time.'

I nod. I don't look up.

'Promise?'

'I promise.' I utter the falsehood a little too brightly. Bryn is my friend; I know I ought to tell him what I am planning to do, but I also know that if I tell him, he will try to stop me.

'Good,' Bryn says. 'And when I've earned a bit o' money, I'll come back to Gosswater to visit you.' He takes my hand again and shakes it firmly. 'Soon.'

'Good luck, Bryn,' I say.

He turns and waves. 'And you, Aggie. An' when you see Sexton Black, tell him . . .' He lifts his chin a little higher. 'Tell him I wish him well.'

I watch as he hobbles away in the snow and, for a moment, I envy the freedom and dignity he has found . . . But I can feel no such forgiveness for Clarence; he and I are on a much darker path.

I turn and walk towards the high, arched doorway of the church.

34

I am aware of how scruffy and dirty I am in my torn coat and my slush-soaked boots, my knees and backside caked in sheep-dung. When I last went to church I was Lady Agatha, impeccably turned out in my Sunday best. I bob a curtsey of apology as I face the altar.

Then I see Thomas, and everything else is pushed out of my head: I call his name – it comes out much louder than I intended, reverberating in the cavernous space. Poor Thomas jumps and spins around. Confusion turns to surprise, then joy. He drops his tools on the stone floor.

'Aggie! What on earth are you doin' here?'

I run to him, relief flooding through me.

He crouches down and holds me gently by the

shoulders. 'How did you get here, bairn? I'm so sorry I couldn't get back to you. I should never have set out with snow on the way. Are you all right?'

I tell him that I tried to walk back from Gosswater village by myself, took the wrong road and ended up sleeping in the sheep shelter at Ramskull Pass. I tell him about Bryn too.

'Bryn Black? He's a good lad that 'un.'

'He is.'

'Well. What an adventure!'

If he only knew the rest of it . . .

'I reckon you need a hot bath and a change o' clothes, lass. Let's get you to the inn.'

'And some food, please,' I add, my stomach gurgling hopefully. 'Will you come with me?'

Thomas looks at his tools. 'Aye, but I won't be able to stay long. There's still so much to do. I'm beginning to wish I'd never taken this on. It's good to be workin' with my hands again, finishin' this job I started, but . . .' He glances at the back of the church, and I turn around to see a very large, pale man sitting in the farthest pew, looking at us.

'Is that the minister?' I whisper. The man's lips are twisted into a cynical sneer. 'The one who offered you the job?'

'Naw. That man's called Hodgson. He's been sent here from the bishop's office.' Thomas turns back to his work.

'Why is he looking at me like that?'

'He's not lookin' at you, lass. He's lookin' at me.'

'Why?'

Thomas frowns. 'Because the bishop wants someone to watch me while I work. Because . . .'

I get a little stabbing pain in my stomach. Somehow I know what he is going to say.

'Because they think I'm goin' to pocket the silver or somethin'.'

Clarence's voice is in my head, whispering: *Thomas Walters is nothing more than a common thief.*

'But, Thomas, you would never . . .'

'O' course I would never. That's not how they see it, though. Give a dog a bad name and hang 'im.' His nostrils flare with anger as he picks up his chisel and begins tapping at a design of two snakes entwined together.

'But that's not fair, Thomas.' We have never spoken of this before – Thomas's reputation as a thief.

His voice is sad rather than angry: ashamed, tired. 'Let me finish this bit o' work, lass, and then I'll take you to the inn.' His eyes flick back to Hodgson, looming there in the shadows. 'Just give me a minute, Aggie.'

I do as he asks and leave him to his work. I walk up and down the church, looking at Thomas's beautiful carvings – more beautiful even than his work on the staircase at Gosswater Hall. All of the animals from the Bible are here – every animal under the sun, in fact. The galleries above are New Testament – the sheep and oxen at Jesus's birth, Mary's donkey, the camels of the kings. The pews in the nave all end with a panel depicting a pair of animals from Noah's ark. I think perhaps I remember some of these designs from when I was small – yes! I remember these lions, these wolves. So, this was Thomas's work: *my father's* work. I feel a tingle of pride. I remember wishing I could choose which pew to sit in – *Shall we be giraffes today, or shall we be elephants?* – instead of always having to sit in our family pew, right up by the pulpit. I go and look at it. No lions for us, no elephants – just the Asquith coat of arms – the geese, the egg and the roses. I can't imagine Clarence making use of this pew very often – once or twice a year, perhaps, to smile and nod at the right sort of people.

I find a door that leads into a little anteroom or vestry, and I slip inside. The walls are lined with huge old books or ledgers, each labelled with a different year. I take one down, blow the dust from it, and look at the cover – *Baptisms, Marriages, Deaths: Year of Our Lord 1851*. That was the year the earl and countess got married. I flick through the pages, trying to decipher the tiny, elaborate writing. June, July . . . Here they are:

August 10th, Henry St John Asquith, Twenty-Ninth Earl of Gosswater, married Miss Catherine Cavendish-Dacre.

I try to imagine my late parents signing this register

on their wedding day – bright-eyed, pink-cheeked twenty-year-olds, not the frail, elderly couple that I knew. I smile. Then I check over my shoulder – I'm sure I'm not meant to be in here. That nasty-looking man, Hodgson, might creep up on me at any minute. I listen for footsteps, but can only hear the tapping of Thomas's hammer.

You should look, Aggie, my brain whispers. *While you have the chance. You should look at 1888.*

My hand trembles as it reaches towards the shelf, towards the year of my birth.

It probably won't be in here – I could have been baptized at any number of churches in the area, and if I was abandoned – left at an orphanage – I might not have been baptized at all . . .

I rest the heavy book on the table in front of me and turn the pages. My heart is pounding and I have a sick feeling in my stomach. January, February, March . . .

What if I see something I don't want to see?

But it is too late. There I am. At least, it must be me. It couldn't possibly be anyone else.

Agatha Rose Walters. Daughter of Thomas Walters and Maud McCarthy (unmarried).

35

I stare at the words in the register, reading them over and over again. I was born out of wedlock. I was baptized. My middle name is Rose. I have Thomas's surname.

And my mother was Maud McCarthy.

Maud McCarthy: the housekeeper at Gosswater Hall.

I cling on to the edge of the desk to stop the room from spinning. My brain tries to take hold of this information, but it slips from my grasp like a wet stone.

Miss McCarthy? The housekeeper at Gosswater Hall?

A noise behind me makes me jump and I almost scream. The door opens and Thomas comes in.

'Aggie – I don't think you're supposed t' . . .' He trails off when he sees my face. 'Aggie? What's wrong?'

I can't speak. My eyes flick back to the register on

the desk and Thomas pushes past me to have a look.

'What's this?'

My shaking finger points at my name.

He stares at the writing. 'But . . .'

The door flies open once more. I slam the register shut and shove it back on the shelf. It's Hodgson.

'Mr Walters . . . Do I take it you have decided to finish your work for the day?' His voice is disdainful, superior.

'No, Mr Hodgson,' Thomas murmurs. 'Aggie just came to – to bring me some tools.'

Hodgson looks me up and down, chewing his bottom lip as if it is pork fat.

'I'm just going to escort her t' the inn,' Thomas goes on. 'Then I'll be back to continue my work. I won't be long.'

'Going to the inn during working hours, eh, Walters?' Hodgson tuts and shakes his head, as if Thomas is a naughty dog. 'The bishop won't be happy to hear that.'

'I'm not going for a drink, sir, I'm takin' the lass there. I'll be as quick as I can.'

'Ten minutes,' Hodgson says. 'Not a second more.' He stands with his back against the open door, so we have to squeeze past him as we leave.

'Not now, Aggie,' Thomas says for the third time. It is the only thing he has said since we left the church. 'We

231

can't talk about it now. It's a long, long story and I've got to be back at the church in five minutes.'

'Please – tell me what happened.'

He stops walking, exasperated. 'Aggie – I wasn't there when you were born or baptized. I didn't know you *existed* until two years ago. I was . . .'

I stop too. 'You were *what*, Thomas?'

'I was in prison.' The truth bursts out of his mouth and I don't know which one of us is more shocked. All the colour has drained from his face.

'For theft?' I whisper.

'For theft,' he spits the words out. 'Aye.' He starts walking again and I struggle to keep up. 'It was a god-awful time. I thought I'd left it all behind – thought we could have a fresh start, you and me, but . . .'

'You knew her, though, Miss McCarthy – Maud – the housekeeper?'

He breathes out, a loud, frustrated sigh. I know I am making him angry, but I can't stop.

'I knew Maud, aye. When I was workin' on the stair-case at Gosswater Hall. She was just a maid then . . . I should talk to her,' he mutters. 'Sort all this out.'

'You can't. Cousin Clarence dismissed her and she's gone back to her family in Ireland.'

He shakes his head. 'Well, that's that, then.' His jaw clamps shut and he walks a bit faster.

'That's *what*, then?'

We're outside the inn now. Thomas stops, takes his

cap off and rubs his forehead hard. From somewhere further down the road a clock strikes the hour. 'I've got to go back now, Aggie – I'm sorry.'

I see him through a blur of frustrated tears.

He looks at me properly for the first time since we left the church, and at last his face softens. 'This isn't the right time, lass. You're tired and hungry, I'm busy wi' my work. We'll talk properly when I've finished this job, Aggie. When we're back home at the cottage. I don't pretend to know all of it, and there are things I don't understand either, but I'll tell you everythin' I know. I promise.'

I nod, but I can't speak. I am too confused, too disappointed. I try to control my tears, breathing hard and gazing beyond Thomas at the grey street. I notice that it is drizzling. It must have been drizzling for a while: most of the snow has melted away and the road is muddy and wet.

A man nods to Thomas from a passing cart. 'Morning, Walters. Have you heard? The pass is clear.'

'Mornin' Bill.' Thomas waves, then turns to me. 'Would you like to go home, Aggie? – After you've had somethin' to eat? Ramskull Pass is clear.'

Is he saying that he wants me to go home without him?

'It's up to you, o' course, but if you go with Bill, you'll be back at the cottage an' into your clean clothes quicker than if you wait for me.' He tries to get a smile out of me. 'And I need someone to feed those geese for me.'

'Very well,' I say quietly. 'I'll go home.'

'If you think you can manage without me a couple more nights, I'll stay here. I can work longer days then and get the job done quicker.'

I nod, but he is already walking away from me. 'I'll see you when I'm finished then,' he calls over his shoulder. 'Two, three days at the most. I'll go and catch Bill and ask him t' wait for you.' He raises his hand in farewell. 'I'm sorry, Aggie. I'll see you soon.' Then he turns and breaks into a run.

It is almost dark by the time I arrive home. Bill nods to me as I hop down from his cart into the melting snow, and I walk down the track to the cottage.

The journey home from town was so different from the journey there: the rattle of the haycart; the rhythmic clopping of the horse's iron shoes on the road; Bill waving and nodding to people as we passed them. There was no danger of getting lost this time.

There was still a lot of snow up at Ramskull Pass – particularly on the fields, and deep drifts on the verges, but the drizzle and the traffic had helped to clear a good track along the road. It might have been a pleasant enough drive, if it hadn't been for the flurry of thoughts in my head, and the frustration too – churning and boiling away.

I go to check on the geese. They rush and honk at me as I open the stable door. I clear away the mucky straw, change their hay and top their troughs up with grain and fresh water. I retrieve the King Stone from beneath Susan. She clacks her beak crossly, as if I have taken an egg from her. 'I'll keep it safe now, Sue,' I say gently. The opal is warm from her feathered belly and, as I polish it on my coat, a constellation of colour shines from its astounding blackness. Its beauty takes my breath away. It has been so many things to me, this stone: an act of defiance; a chosen inheritance; a little piece of the world I have left behind. The King Stone has been my secret symbol of power – something for me to cling to while everything else has changed and shifted and fallen away. Now, as I ready myself for the battle ahead, its brilliant blackness reminds me that I have beaten Clarence once, and I can beat him again. I wrap it in my handkerchief and put it safely in my pocket.

I close the shed door and make my way back to the cottage, carefully clutching two warm goose eggs for my supper. The evening shadows are deep and cold. Something rustles in the undergrowth, and I freeze, scanning the leaves for movement.

Fox? Yes – there he is! He is carrying a large bird in his mouth – a moorhen, I think. He must have taken it as it roosted on the bank of the lake. He stops and stares back at me, his eyes flashing like jewels, then he blinks and takes his prey into the bushes. I am sorry for the poor bird, but I am glad that Fox survived the hunt and the snow, and that he will be eating well tonight.

'Good night, Fox,' I whisper.

I go into the bright kitchen and lock the door behind me. When I look out through the window the sky seems suddenly, impossibly dark. Night has spread its raven wings.

The kind lady at the inn in Penrith gave me a basket of bread, milk and butter, so along with the fresh goose eggs I am able to cobble together a good meal. I sit by the parlour fire with the plate on my lap. I need to be strong and rested for tomorrow, and I need to have a clear head. I try to think my way through the muddle of thoughts stupefying my poor brain.

Maud McCarthy? It is as if my brain is still reading that page in the register. *Maud McCarthy?*

I try to press this piece of the jigsaw puzzle into place. Thomas is my father and Miss McCarthy is my mother. They met while he was working on the staircase at Gosswater Hall. *But . . . BUT!* my brain cries out, infuriated. Why wouldn't they have married? Why did she give me up to the earl and countess to be raised as an Asquith?

Thomas will be able to answer some of these questions when he returns, I hope, but it seems there are things even he doesn't know. I feel sure the letter mentioned in the earl's will holds the key to the mystery. And, if my plan works tomorrow, those 'shameful secrets' of the past will soon be in my hands . . .

36

In a moment I'll get up, and go upstairs, and wash, and brush my teeth, and put on my nightgown and go to bed . . . I do all these things in my head several times without leaving my chair. I hear the pop and crackle of wood burning and realize I am still sitting beside the parlour fire. My supper plate is still on my lap. In a moment I'll get up, and put my plate in the kitchen, and go upstairs, and wash, and brush my teeth, and put on my nightgown . . .

But I am too tired to move. The fire slowly dies. The room cools and darkens, and still I am there sliding in and out of sleep.

I am on a stage in a theatre, trying to recite lines from a play that I can't quite remember. The audience are silent as corpses, staring at me empty-eyed. *Who am I?*

I am the ghost. Yes – I am dressed in a silver crown and a long white robe and I must tell Hamlet to kill Cousin Clarence . . . I try to raise my hands, but I can't move them. When I look, I see they aren't real hands at all – they are made of cloth. Strings are threaded through my cloth palms and my hands move only when the strings are pulled. I look up and see, towering above me, the figure who has made a puppet of me – it is a huge skeleton, taller than the castle behind us, much taller – the skeleton of a giant. He looks down at me and laughs. His skull is not a human skull, but it is familiar – *I knew him, Horatio* . . . He has sharp, curling horns either side of his narrow muzzle and he grins down at me . . .

I am woken by the striking of the clock. I jump up and there is a clatter and crash as the plate slides from my lap and smashes on the flagstone floor. *One o'clock in the morning.* I smell the faintest trace of roses in the air. *Has she been here, the Ghost Girl?* I blink and blink – there seem to be echoes of light on my eyelids, as if something flared up in front of me and then vanished again. Perhaps Rose had something to do with that terrible dream. It felt like a warning . . .

It was just a dream, Aggie. Just a dream.

I go upstairs, and wash, and brush my teeth, and put on my nightgown and go to bed.

By the time I arrive at Gosswater Hall the next morning, every nerve in my body is awake and alert and buzzing. I knock at the door.

There is no answer. I wait for some time. Clarence obviously hasn't hired any new servants yet. I walk around the side of the house, my eyes wide open, my ears pricked up, wary of Brutus charging towards me, but he is nowhere to be seen.

Then I see Clarence – a forlorn figure in the morning mist. He is stooped over a flower bed, sifting handfuls of dirt through his bare fingers. Uprooted rose bushes are strewn amongst the muddy patches of snow on the wet grass.

'Good morning, Clarence,' I call, determined to have the upper hand from the very start. He straightens up. His eyes are glowing coals in a face ashen with exhaustion. He is caked in mud from head to toe.

'*A rose bush*, Cousin Agatha?' He staggers towards me. '*Father loved the garden*,' he whines, mocking my voice. 'I've dug up every blasted rose bush on the whole estate, and do you know what I've found?'

'What have you found, Clarence?'

'NOTHING! I've found NOTHING!' He bellows the words in my face and I have to close my eyes against the stench of his breath.

I force a polite smile. 'Sorry. I was just trying to help, Clarence. I see now that I made a mistake, but I can put that right. I know exactly where the Queen Stone is. I'm certain this time.'

He steps even closer, so that his muddy shoes are

toe-to-toe with my mine. '*Are* you, Agatha? Are you really?' His wild eyes search my face. 'Then you can take me to it right now, can't you?'

'Very well.'

Clarence blinks. He didn't think it was going to be this easy.

I set off towards the lake. 'We'll need to take a boat.'

Clarence's face lights up. 'Aha! An island! The very place for buried treasure . . .' His eyes are different now – glazed with greed, as if he is already holding the opal in his filthy hands. He starts walking too.

I stop. 'Oh – there's just one more thing, Clarence.'

'What's that?'

'I want something from you in return. I'll show you where the Queen Stone is hidden if you give me the earl's letter. The one that he mentions in the will.'

Clarence narrows his eyes, his loose lips curl with disdain. 'I never should have let you get your little paws on that will.'

'If you give me the letter, you get the Queen Stone. It's that simple. I can wait here while you go and get it. It should have been attached to the will.'

Clarence looks confused for a moment, then he rummages in his pocket and pulls out a crumpled envelope. 'This one?' He holds it up. It is wax-sealed with the earl's stamp, just like the will. It is addressed to Mr Thomas Walters of Goss Farm and marked PRIVATE.

That must be it! I stretch out my hand, but Clarence

holds it up beyond my reach.

'Ought to have passed this on to your *father*, but, to be perfectly honest with you, I forgot all about it. It can't be all that important, can it? What business would the late earl have had with a lowly, ne'er-do-well goose farmer? Just some sentimental nonsense about you, I would have thought? Unless . . .' He looks at me more carefully, suddenly sensing the value of this bargaining chip. 'It *is* important, isn't it, Agatha? If you're willing to give me the Queen Stone for it . . .'

'It's important for Thomas, and for me. It is nothing to you.'

'Not quite nothing. This is my payment for the opal. Fair and square.' He puts the envelope, now covered in his muddy fingerprints, back in his pocket. 'You can have your precious letter when I've got my Queen Stone.'

He holds out his dirty hand and I shake it, shuddering inwardly. 'Let's go, then,' I say.

37

We walk across the estate to the jetty. Clarence is humming and singing beneath his breath: 'A-hunting we will go, a-hunting we will go . . .' His manic mood is unnerving. I try to focus on the plan, rehearsing every step in my head over and over.

I get a shock when we arrive at the jetty and find Sexton Black there, unloading a large spade from what is unmistakably Thomas's rowing boat. 'Ah! Yer Lordship!' he calls. 'I got that there shovel. Always happy to help an important man like yerself.' He bows greasily. 'For due payment, o' course.'

'Change of plan, Sexton,' Clarence says, gesturing for me to climb aboard and following close behind. 'We are going on a boat trip with my friend Agatha here. And you can row us. Where are we going, Agatha?'

'Skelter Island.'

Sexton Black sees me properly for the first time. '*You* again?' he hisses. 'Like a bad penny, aren't yer?'

'She is, isn't she.' Clarence mutters. Then: 'Sexton Black called here at the Hall yesterday, looking for — what was it you were looking for?'

'The boy,' Sexton Black growls. 'The wicked runaway boy . . .'

'That's right. And he kindly offered to help me with my digging.'

The sexton nods eagerly. 'I'm good at diggin' holes,' he says, putting the spade back into the boat and pushing us off from the jetty. 'For due payment, o' course, yer Lordship.'

'Quite.'

Sexton Black's face spreads into a toothless grimace. Something from my dream flashes through my mind — the grinning skull, the puppeteer. I feel cold all over.

Clarence is still humming to himself, reclining in the bow and trailing a hand in the freezing water as if it is a summer's day. With each stroke I feel a greater sense of dread. Is he going to throw me into the lake?

He can't do that — he needs you to show him where the treasure is. He won't hurt you while he thinks you're still useful to him . . .

Clarence's stupid song is chiming in my head — *A-hunting we will go, a-hunting we will go* — and for some reason I can't stop thinking about that old riddle with the fox and the chicken and the grain. It's something about being here in the boat with greedy Cousin Clarence and sly Sexton Black. You can't leave the chicken with the grain, you can't leave the fox with the chicken . . .

The mist hangs over the water like a funeral pall. I can't see the island ahead, and I can barely see the land behind us. At one point, I think I hear a voice — from the direction of Thomas's cottage — someone calling my name. I turn quickly, but there is nothing to see. The mist has swallowed everything up and the voice has gone.

Just ducks, probably.

Right on cue, the quacking of mallards resounds over the water like cruel laughter. Skelter Island looms into view.

My face is set in a smile, as if I am quietly in control, but it is getting harder and harder to pretend that this is the case. *Think of the geese, Aggie — gliding gracefully on the surface of the lake, feet paddling madly out of sight. You can do this. Don't let Clarence see you are afraid.*

I lead the way to Rose's tomb.

'Thank you, Sexton,' I say, in what used to be Lady Agatha's voice. 'That will be all.'

I hold my breath. *Has it worked?*

The sexton leers at me. Then he doffs his cap to Clarence. 'Yer Lordship,' he oozes. He turns away, and limps off through the trees towards his shack.

Clarence turns to me. 'So, little cousin. Where is the treasure?'

I take a deep breath and point at the rose etched into the silver birch. 'Look,' I say. '*The eternal rose*. This is Rose Asquith's tomb. The earl hid the Queen Stone in here.'

Clarence studies the rose. He breathes heavily. 'Yes,' he whispers. 'Yes – in here.'

I open the door to the tomb and step back. 'Give me the letter,' I say, 'and I'll tell you exactly where you need to look.'

Clarence's gaze is strangely steady, as if he is suddenly one step ahead of me.

'Why don't you go in and get it for me, Agatha, and then I'll give you the letter?' he says with a smirk.

Hold your nerve, Aggie – just hold your nerve.

I shake my head. 'The letter first,' I say, hoping that my voice sounds more confident to him than it does to me.

He contorts his face into an expression of mock-sadness. 'Oh, dear little Agatha – we appear to be at a stalemate, don't we?'

'The letter,' I demand. And I hold my hand out for it.

'Oh, this?' Clarence says, taking the envelope from his pocket and waving it around in a casual fashion. 'Is this what you want?'

'You know it is.' I'm not playing his game; he's meant to be playing *mine*.

He reaches into another pocket and pulls out a box of matches.

No . . .

He strikes a match. Then he holds the burning flame just beneath the corner of the envelope.

'Clarence, don't! We made a bargain—'

'Yes, yes, little cousin.' He is smiling again. The edge of the paper is starting to blacken. 'How's this for a bargain? Go in there and get the Queen Stone for me and I won't burn the letter.'

'Clarence, you can't burn it! Stop!'

The flame has caught hold of the paper now.

'Clarence, STOP!'

I rush at him, but then – from out of the shadows – Sexton Black returns, armed with his huge, rusty pitchfork. He jabs the sharp prongs at me and I step back.

Clarence drops the flaming letter on the ground, and I stare helplessly as it burns, and blackens, and crumbles into ash.

This was not part of the plan. It was not meant to happen like this.

'Thank you, Sexton,' Clarence says. 'Wild little

thing, aren't you, Agatha? Wild and deceitful.'

I am so furious I cannot speak. It's gone – the letter is gone. The truth is lost . . .

'I could see your ruse written all over your face. You were going to tempt me into the tomb with the promise of treasure, and then you were going to lock me in there, weren't you?'

'I . . .' I don't know what to say. There seems to be little point denying any of it now. My plan has been found out.

'You've dreamt about it, haven't you? The feeling of revenge as you slam the door and slide the bolt home. The delicious satisfaction of knowing that I'm going to die a slow and miserable death, alone in the stinking darkness. That's what you wanted, wasn't it?'

'Yes,' I say, holding my stubborn chin high. 'That's exactly what I wanted.'

'It's remarkable, really,' Clarence says wistfully, his head on one side.

'What is?'

'That you're not an Asquith after all. We're just so *alike*, Agatha!'

He steps towards me, arms outstretched, herding me towards the door of the tomb.

'Clarence, don't . . .'

I try to move to the side, back on to the path, but Sexton Black is there, prodding at me with the fork. He is cackling to himself as if he's never had this much fun. 'Nasty little children,' he hisses. 'Sinful an' wicked – you an' that Bryn – one as bad as t' other. Need t' be taught a lesson.'

I've only got one chance: I try to make a run for it, ducking under Clarence's arm, but he trips me up and I fall flat on my stomach on to a slab of stone. The breath is thumped out of my body and I hear a hard clunk, followed by something that sounds like a large marble rolling across a stone floor. My hand goes straight to my coat pocket. Empty! I twist around just in time to see the King Stone spinning across the silvery floor, into the darkness of the tomb.

'YOU HAD IT! My opal! You *thief* – you thieving *witch*!' Clarence yanks me up by the scruff of my coat – the buttons at the neck cut into my throat and I can hardly breathe. 'Get it! Get that stone, Sexton!'

Sexton Black scurries into the tomb and comes out holding the King Stone aloft, all agog. He spits on it and rubs it on his dirty jacket.

Clarence hauls me into the marble doorway. 'Last chance to tell me the truth: is the Queen Stone in there or not, you foul little harpy?'

'No, it's not! I don't know where it is!' I scream back. 'And it's not yours, anyway! You'll never be the real Earl of Gosswater – the Queen Stone was left to ME!'

'Then *you* can spend eternity LOOKING FOR IT!' Clarence bellows. He grabs the sexton's pitchfork from him and jabs at me hard to force me into the tomb. I stumble backwards, losing my balance. The back of my head cracks into the edge of the stone table and I cry out, falling to the floor.

The sexton cackles, and in that dizzy flash of pain I see something strange: all around him I see a swarm of spirits, black as bats – cruel and dark as the thundering sky. *Are these the ghosts he spoke of? The sinful souls of the island, haunting and tormenting him day and night?*

The door to the tomb is closing. I crawl forwards and push with both hands, throwing all my weight against it, but it is no use. The last thing I see in the narrowing slit of daylight is my beautiful King Stone – gleaming like the eye of midnight itself – in Sexton Black's filthy hands.

Then the whole world goes dark.

And I hear the bolt drawn smoothly into place.

38

Just me, and the blackness, and my breathing . . .

Now what?

Silence.

Well?

I don't think there's any getting out of this, Aggie.

This is how it ends?

Yes. I think so.

I am starting to feel faint and shaky, and I can't tell if it's the blow to the head, or the terrifying certainty that death is coming for me . . . The pain has dulled to a heavy, insistent throbbing. The darkness pools in front of my eyes like spilt ink and suddenly I have no strength in my body at all. My eyes close as I slump on to the cold floor.

It isn't sleep, it is unconsciousness – sinking down

through an endless black silence, deep and peaceful as the midnight lake, far away from the world above; down, down into an ever deeper darkness. I am drifting for hours, days perhaps. Time means nothing now. At least there is no more pain.

I don't feel afraid, and I don't feel alone either.

There is a soft light ahead.

Death, perhaps? It is kinder than I thought it would be. A gentle, ghostly glow, like a lamp far away in the fog.

There are water-cool fingers stroking my hair . . .

I gasp. The sensation is real. It drags me back into my body, up from the deep black lake, surging suddenly towards the light, darkness dripping from me as I surface. I am back in the tomb, panting for air, blinking with pain – but She is here. My sister Rose is here with me.

And then someone is calling my name . . .

Footsteps outside – the voice calling again, closer now:

'Aggie? Aggie, are you in there?'

It can't be . . .

Bryn?

The bolt is drawn back. The door shifts, creaks and opens.

'Aggie!'

I open my eyes and am blinded by the light of his lantern – I squint into Bryn's upside-down face.

'Aggie – are you hurt? Where are you hurt?'

'My head,' I murmur. Unconsciousness is dragging at me; each breath feels like work.

I feel Bryn's hands. He is pulling me up to sitting and heaving me on to my feet.

'I can't walk, Bryn.'

'You can, Aggie. You have to.'

'Where are we going?'

'We're gettin' off this cursed island. We're gettin' you some help.'

I am aware of Bryn's arm around me, my feet staggering along the wet path, the blaring pain in my head. It is the middle of the night now – the earth is black, the trees are black, everything is cold.

I can hear a voice behind us – the sexton? Did he hear us? See the light? Was he waiting for Bryn to come back?

'Faster, Aggie.'

I try to move my legs faster, but I trip and Bryn has to catch me in both his arms.

The sexton is screaming at us – threats and curses.

'Go to hell, Sexton Black,' I breathe.

'He's already there,' Bryn says.

I think of those cruel dark spirits swarming around him – haunting, whispering, tormenting. *Yes. He is.*

We are at the water's edge. Bryn lifts me into the boat as if I weigh no more than a lamb. 'Hang on, Aggie.' He pushes the boat out into the water. The voice of the sexton is faint now. He has given up the chase. I try to breathe, focusing on the pulsing of my blood, the splashing of the oars. My bones are aching and cold. I can feel the dampness of the night air settling on my face, my eyelids.

'Keep your eyes open, Aggie – I'll get you help.'

Cool fingers are still stroking my hair. A hand of mist holds mine.

Bryn is rowing hard. The waves slap the bow. I hear the rush, rush of the black lake beneath us – shhhhh, shhhhh – like Rose's lullaby. Such beautiful music . . .

'Aggie, please. Try to keep your eyes open.'

But the darkness is kind and it is opening its arms to me.

I am woken by a very strange sound – a mewling, like a hungry little animal.

There is a woman's voice too – crooning softly – and I can feel the warmth of a fire on my skin. My bones no longer feel cold. I feel warm all the way through. Warm and safe. The pillow beneath my cheek is liquid-soft. Satin. I am back in Gosswater Hall – I must be . . .

'She's awake.' A different woman's voice – older this time.

'Is she all right?'

Bryn.

'I'm all right,' I murmur. When I open my eyes, I see

where I am. I am at Moll Speedwell's castle. And here she is, sitting beside me.

'You've had a bad bump, child, yer exhausted and you've had a nasty fright, but you'll be right as rain after a bit o' rest and some hot food.'

I sit up. My head spins and Bryn steadies me, tucking a cushion behind my back to prop me up.

'How long have I been asleep?'

'Hours of the night and hours of the mornin'.' Moll takes my hands and carefully gives me a steaming bowl of broth – it smells very strange. 'This will help,' she says.

'What is it?'

'Mutton and marigold.' She laughs, as if she can see the face I am pulling.

I take sips of the broth from a silver spoon and look around, dazed by the extraordinary colours of Moll's home.

That mewling sound again. I turn and see Ivy Speedwell. And there, tucked closely against her chest, is a tiny baby, all wrapped up in a blanket.

'Oh! You had your baby, Ivy!'

Ivy laughs. 'Yes – came as a bit of a surprise to me, too – he's early. The pains started when I was on my way here in the boat yesterday and I stayed with Moll so she could help me. We couldn't have been in better hands, could we, my darling boy?'

'Does he have a name?'

'Not yet.'

'Bryn,' says Bryn. 'Bryn is an excellent name. A hero's name.'

Ivy laughs and so do I.

'Thank you for rescuing me, Bryn,' I say quietly.

'Well, it were only fair – after you rescued me from Ramskull Pass.' And he gives me a wink.

'But how did you know I was there on the island? I thought you were going to stay in Penrith.'

'Well. I had a feelin' you were up to summat. I didn't believe you for a moment when you said you'd let things lie. I spent the night in town – my pal's ma stuffed me with food and strapped me ankle up for me. Then I caught a lift back to the village yesterday mornin' on the brewery cart. I come to find you at the cottage, and thought I saw you out on the water – in a boat with the sexton an' that cousin of yours. That don't bode well, I said to meself. I called to you, but the mist was closin' in . . .'

'I heard you.' I smile.

'Any road, there was no boat there, so I had to hitch a ride back to the village and walk to where I'd hidden the sexton's boat. Didn't get to the island till nightfall, then I had to wait until Sexton Black had stopped wandering around . . . I'm just sorry I took so long to get t' you.'

'I'm glad you didn't believe me,' I say.

'I'm fairly glad o' that too,' Bryn twinkles. 'And I'm

glad you're all right.'

'But how did you know I was in Rose's tomb?'

'There were a light – I followed it through the trees. Must've been an oil lamp or summat left there . . .'

'There wasn't a lamp. It was daylight when Clarence locked me in . . .'

Our eyes meet as we both realize: the Ghost Girl saved me – she led Bryn to the tomb. We share a dazed smile.

The baby cries again and Ivy feeds him. I watch the baby gazing up at her, his tiny hand gripping her finger. For some reason, I feel tears starting in my eyes, a soft ache in my throat.

Ivy looks at me and smiles. 'I've asked her,' she says, nodding at Old Moll. 'About what you mentioned the other day – your mother. I've asked Moll to tell you what she knows.'

I swallow. 'But you said you made a promise, Moll. You said you'd lose everything . . .'

Moll waves a hand. 'Hush,' she says. Then she stands up and puts a hand out. Ivy guides her to sit down beside her, and puts the tiny baby into Moll's arms. '*This* is everythin'. He's a beauty, isn't he?' Moll whispers, as if she can see his round, pink cheeks, his rosebud mouth. She gazes at him through eyes milky as pearls. Her fingertips move gently over his tiny nose, his brow, the tuft of fine hair on his head. 'You got me thinkin', child. You an' that lawyer fellow with his papers. I didn't sign 'em in the end. I've had more money than I can spend for over ten year and kep' the secret all that time. What good can come from keepin' it another ten year? What good is a castle,' she says softly, 'if you sit in it alone?'

'Moll's going to come back with me,' Ivy says. 'She's going to patch up the fight with Dad and live with us in the village, aren't you, Moll? Help me look after this little chap.'

'But I thought you wanted to end your days as a queen, Moll.'

'I am. I will. Look at me,' and she kisses the baby on his forehead. 'Right now, I'm the richest woman in the world.'

Ivy is smiling at her, and there are tears in her eyes too.

'An' there's only so much Turkish Delight an old lady can eat, after all.'

We are all smiling now. I notice Bryn has a large box of chocolates on his lap. He offers them to me and I take one. The sweet warmth spreads through me.

'Would you like me to tell you now?' Moll says, carefully passing the sleeping baby back to his mother. 'Or d'you want to wait until you're feelin' stronger?'

Now, please, my brain says quickly – impatient as ever. The rest of me is hesitating. After wanting to know for all this time, I don't know if I am ready . . .

'How much do you know?' Moll asks.

I take a deep breath and tell her about my childhood at Gosswater Hall with the earl and countess, and about Cousin Clarence making me leave to go and live with Thomas. I tell her what Father wrote in his will. And I tell her about the record of baptism I found in the church.

Bryn did not know this last part of the story – his eyes are big as moons. Old Moll shakes her head. 'What a tangle,' she says. 'What a sad, sad tangle.'

'What is?'

'Oh – all of it. An' it could've been such a simple, happy tale. But other things got in the way. Cold things, like shame and fear.'

She isn't making sense. 'Tell me,' I beg. 'Please, Moll. Just tell me.'

She smiles again. 'You have her voice,' she says. 'Exactly the same voice as Rose – soft as a lullaby.'

'You knew my sister Rose?'

'Yes, I knew her.' And she pauses, looking right at me with her kind, blind eyes. 'But she wasn't your sister, child. Rose was your mother.'

39

'Rose was born to the earl and countess when they had given up hope of having a child,' says Moll. 'She were the most precious thing in their world, always dressed in the most beautiful, expensive clothes – they gave her anythin' and everythin' she wanted. Most children raised like that would've grown up to be selfish and lazy, not knowin' the value o' things or people, but Rose had the sweetest nature. And she were wild as the wind – just wanted to be out on the fells, or swimmin' in the lake.

'She were seventeen when Thomas Walters come to repair the staircase at Gosswater Hall. He were apprentice to the carpenters in Penrith at the time. Just a lad, but so talented – a born artist. He and Rose fell in love like it was the most natural thing in the whole world. Which it were, if you ask me – but not for the earl and countess, o' course. When Rose said she wanted to marry Thomas Walters, she might as well've said she wanted to marry a sheep dog. The earl told her it were out o' the question – not only was the boy beneath her, but he didn't trust him either. Said he thought the lad were a bad lot. Rose didn't believe him, o' course, an' the poor lass fell to pieces when Thomas were sent to prison for stealin' the jewel.'

'The Queen Stone?' I breathe, transfixed.

Moll nods. 'Aye. Thomas Walters stole the Queen Stone from Gosswater Hall, and he were put in prison. They never did find it.'

I stare at her, frozen – I can't believe what I'm hearing.

'O' course the earl and countess did their best to keep the whole thing hushed up, and it were just as well. Not long after Thomas were sent down, Rose was found to be with child. The earl and countess hid her away from the world – hoping to protect her reputation. She might still have had a chance of marryin' well, yer see, if they could keep it secret and give the babby away. But poor Rose started to sicken. I've never seen anythin' like it. Not an infection or a fever or anything I knew. It were as if she just turned her back on life. People talked about the curse o' the Queen Stone, but it were a broken heart that did for her. Rather than gettin' one of their expensive doctors from town, the earl and countess called for me. And they gave me money – so much money – if I promised that I would never speak a word of it to anyone.' She smiles to herself and shakes her head. 'Ah, well. So much for that. When the time come for you to be born, Rose just wasn't strong enough. She never recovered from the delivery. Oh! She loved you, though, child. You were the only thing she saw – the only thing that mattered. Even when she were weak as water, she'd still get out o' bed and climb up the back stairs to the nursery just to hold you and sing to you. She was found there on the staircase one morning – cold as stone. She'd been tryin' to come to you one last time.'

Tears are running down my face. Moll's small hand takes mine, and Ivy passes me a handkerchief.

'The earl and countess had planned to send you to th' orphanage, but wi' Rose gone, they couldn't bear to lose you too. You were all they had left. They were far too old then to pass you off as their own – folks would have known it were a lie – so the countess had the idea of getting young Maud McCarthy to have you baptized and registered as hers. Paid her a fair amount for her trouble too, and she were promoted from maid to housekeeper. She wanted to stay at the Hall to look after you.

'Adopting a baby girl when they'd just lost their own daughter was convincin' enough for folk, and it would all've worked like a dream if you hadn't grown up to look so much like Rose. Well – that's what Maud said.' Moll reaches out towards me and cups my face in her palm for a moment. 'Yes. So like her.'

I am smiling through my tears.

'The older you got, the more the earl and countess had to keep you out of sight. If anyone had guessed the truth – that their perfect Rose had a child out o' wedlock – they'd have died o' shame. They made sure the rest o' the family was kept away from Gosswater – kept away from you . . .'

I think about Great-aunt Millicent at the earl's funeral – the shock on her face when she saw me standing there in the mist: a shock that stopped her heart dead. She must have thought she was looking at Rose – a girl she knew to have died twelve years before. A ghost girl.

'And they couldn't let you guess the truth either,' Moll goes on. 'That's why they kept it all from you.'

Memories are fluttering around me like moths – rising and quivering in the air and settling somewhere new: the same and yet different. Things are beginning to make sense. I have answers to things I hadn't even known were questions. Why they were so protective of me and couldn't bear me doing dangerous things like horse-riding or swimming in the lake; why they loved me but couldn't bear to look at me; why we hardly ever saw anyone. Why I spent my childhood in a gilded cage . . .

'The earl and countess were my grandparents,' I say at last. So I *do* have Asquith blood in my veins; a stubborn Asquith chin.

'Yes, child.'

'And Thomas . . .'

'Well. He'll tell you his part in his own good time. All I know is, he didn't know anythin' about you until he were released from prison. When he heard about the child at Gosswater Hall, he guessed the truth. He tried to see you, but the earl and countess wouldn't let him near. Kept him from his own daughter. Until—'

'Until Clarence read the earl's will, realized he could get rid of me, and turfed me out of Gosswater Hall.'

'From what you say, it seems that your grandfather had some doubts on his death bed. Perhaps in the end he weren't so afraid of the truth.'

'Yes.' I think she is right. And that's not all . . . 'I think Rose wants me to know the truth too.'

'Rose does?' Moll frowns.

'Yes.'

Bryn looks at me. *You're going to tell her about the Ghost Girl?* his eyes say.

But I don't have to. Old Moll looks up, her blind, opal-white eyes staring at the space just behind me. The back of my neck tingles.

'Yes,' Moll whispers. 'Yes, I believe she does.'

40

'**Y**ou *can't* open it, Aggie,' Bryn says again. 'It's addressed to Thomas.'

'I know,' I say, staring at the white envelope in my hands. It is all I can do to stop my fingers from breaking the wax seal.

We have returned to Thomas's cottage late in the afternoon to find a formal calling card on the doormat along with an envelope identical to the one Cousin Clarence burnt before me on Skelter Island.

'Read the message again, please, Bryn,' I say, not taking my eyes off the envelope in my quivering hands. 'And it's definitely today's date?'

'Aye. It is.' Bryn holds the calling card up and reads it aloud:

For the attention of Miss Agatha,

I am sorry to have found the cottage empty when I called for you here these past two days. I should very much like to talk to you in order to be satisfied that the late earl's wishes have been respected. I know he was anxious about your welfare and your future. I will be visiting Gosswater Hall this evening, should you be available to call and find me there. I am also delivering herewith the official copy of the personal letter from the late earl to Mr Thomas Walters, as I suspect that the original letter has not yet been passed on by the executor, Lord Clarence. Please ensure this finds its way to Mr Walters without delay.

Regards,

Charles Hetherington

Hetherington, Amos and Tully

I smooth the envelope carefully and place it on the kitchen table, then I pick it up again immediately. I am not letting it out of my sight until I can put it into Thomas's hands. *Two, three days at the most*, he said when we parted in Penrith. He'll be home by tomorrow.

You've waited this long to hear the truth in the earl's own words, Aggie; you can wait one more day . . .

'I'll go,' I say. 'To Gosswater Hall, to talk to Mr Hetherington.'

Bryn gawps at me: 'Are you mad? Clarence tried t' kill you – he left you locked up in a tomb! You can't just turn up at his house like a dinner guest!'

'He won't dare harm me in front of Mr Hetherington.

And anyway – you'll be there to protect me, won't you, Bryn?'

He folds his arms. 'You need to rest, Aggie – Moll said so. And my ankle's still too sore to walk that far.'

'I feel a lot better. And we don't need to walk. We can take your boat to the Gosswater Hall jetty. Bryn, please – Mr Hetherington needs to know what Clarence has done.'

Bryn shakes his head at me. 'Nope. It's a bad idea.'

'Oh, you're impossible, Bryn!'

'Just lookin' out for you, Aggie. Someone needs to.'

I huff quietly, toying with the envelope in my hands. My thumbnails pick at the edges of the wax seal; they leave a pattern of little half-moons around the Asquith crest – the Queen Stone, the geese and the roses: *In aeternum fidelis*.

The geese, and the roses, eternally loyal . . .

'Oh, heavens, Bryn.' I leap up. 'I understand!'

'Understand what? Wait, Aggie! Where are you goin'?'

Halfway up the stairs already, I turn and shout back at him: 'To get dressed for dinner, Bryn!'

'But—'

'No buts! You and I are going to Gosswater Hall! We are going to tell Mr Hetherington the truth about Clarence – *and* . . .' I take a big excited breath.

'*And* what?'

'And we are going to get the Queen Stone!'

The journey across the water is black and bitterly cold.
I am wearing the blue silk dress I wore when I was sent
away from Gosswater Hall. It somehow feels right that
I am wearing it tonight – there is a sort of dark symmetry to it. Bryn is wearing a black coat that we found in
Thomas's cupboard – it is much too big for him – and
a scarf as a sort of tie or cravat. It is the closest thing to
evening dress we could manage. He stared at himself in
the mirror, smoothing down his lapels. I told him he
looked marvellous, and he blushed.

We moor up at the Gosswater Hall jetty, and Bryn
takes the oil lamp from the boat, lighting our way as we
walk across the estate to the house. He thinks this is a
terrible idea, but he wouldn't let me come by myself,
and I feel so much stronger for having him here beside
me. Lights are blazing from the rooms on the ground
floor – just as they did on New Year's Eve. I can almost
feel the heat of the fires – warmer with every step we
take. I think of the wood and oil and candles Clarence
is squandering, and I see that the Gosswater estate will
not last long in his hands. He will gorge himself on his
riches; he will lose everything.

We walk through wet grass and patches of snow,
past the churned-up rose beds, around the side of the
house to the front door. We cross the bridge over the
moat and go up the steps . . .

There is no answer when we ring the bell. *Still no*

staff? How can he be hosting a party without cooks or maids or footmen? It is very odd, and dreadfully quiet. Eventually I push at the door and it opens slowly to reveal the bare stones of the atrium, glowing gold in the firelight. There is no sign of Clarence.

'Summat feels wrong, Aggie,' Bryn whispers. 'We should go.'

Noises from the dining room – cutlery on crockery, the pop of a champagne cork.

I shake my head. 'He's in there. With Mr Hetherington, I should think. They can't have heard the bell.'

Bryn starts down the corridor.

'No – wait, Bryn,' I hiss. 'There's something we need to do first.'

I go up the stairs, greeting Thomas's beautiful carvings with the palm of my hand. I stop on the landing and turn to face the Asquith shield. There is my King Stone, back in its mount. Bryn has only seen it in the darkness of the goose shed; now he holds his oil lamp up and the opal gleams at us with its mysterious colours. I quickly look over the balustrade, but there is no sign of Clarence. With a juddering heart, I turn my attention to the banner on the shield, engraved with the family motto:

IN AETERNUM FIDELIS

Thorny tendrils and blooms are entwined about the word *aeternum*.

'The eternal rose,' I whisper.

'What?'

'Something my grandfather said before he died –
The eternal rose. I saw the earl's seal on the envelope and
I suddenly knew . . .' I move my fingers carefully
around the carving.

Then there is a voice from the atrium: 'You're nearly
there, Aggie.' My heart lurches and I gasp. We both spin
around, but it isn't Clarence. *Thank goodness.*

'Thomas!' I feel that familiar flood of relief – just as
I felt when I saw him in Penrith church. *Thomas feels
like home.*

He strides across the hallway and takes the stairs
three at a time.

'Finished the job this afternoon and came straight
back, just as I promised. I saw that card on the kitchen
table and thought I'd better come and find you.' He
looks at me closely. 'Are you all right? And you, Bryn?
You two shouldn't've come here without me.'

'I'm all right. I'm so glad you're here, Thomas.'

'Aye. It's strange to be here after all this time,
though.' He looks around and shivers. 'Clarence
Asquith can burn all the fires he likes – he won't be
able to make the darkness in this place go away.'

I know exactly what he means.

Then he reaches towards the shield above us.
'You're lookin' for the earl's safe, are you? The secret
compartment?'

'Yes.' I hold my breath.

Thomas nods. 'I made it for him. Here,' he says quietly. His hand moves across the design it created all those years ago. I see now that one rose bloom is smaller than the rest, deeper set. His fingers press into it and there is a heavy click. A jigsaw-piece of the shield swings open like a door and I see the secret cavity within.

'By . . .' Bryn breathes.

'There's something in there,' I say, looking into the dark little hidey-hole. I reach in and my fingers close around a small, heavy bag. The things inside shift and clink like coins or glass. The cloth is a very fine, soft silk – pearl-white – drawn together at the top with a thin cord.

'Treasure!' says Bryn, as I open the bag, his eyes round as sovereigns. And he's right – a diamond necklace sparkling like white fire; a blindingly blue sapphire tiara; a ruby ring, red as blood. These are the countess's jewels, the ones my grandfather mentioned in his will.

'And there's summat else . . .' Bryn reaches in this time, holding up his lamp with the other hand. He takes out a dark case – about the size of an egg box – with a little jewelled handle and a diamond clasp.

My heart starts to thud. I give the jewels to Bryn to hold and he passes me the case.

I take a deep breath and click the clasp open.

41

Inside, the box is lined with blue silk. Something precious lies cradled here. Something luminous and extraordinary.

'The Queen Stone!' I whisper.

It is more beautiful than anything I have ever seen – more subtle than diamonds, more magical. The white opal glows with a weird, ghostly light – a perfect moon, a will-o'-the-wisp. As I turn it in the lamplight, I see fiery rainbows trapped in ice; aurora dancing in a globe of snow.

'It was here?' Thomas says very quietly. I drag my eyes from the opal's eerie beauty and see the pain and confusion on Thomas's face as he stares and stares. 'They said I'd stolen it – I was sent to *prison* for stealin' it – but it was *here* all along?'

He was innocent. Of course he was. I don't know what to say. And then I remember the letter. 'Perhaps you should read this, Thomas,' I whisper. I give him the envelope from my coat pocket. 'It's something the earl wanted to say to you before he died.'

He opens the envelope, his hands suddenly clumsy.

'What does it say?'

His voice is taut as he reads the letter out loud.

Mr Walters,

Please forgive my cowardice in writing this down rather than talking to you face to face. I cannot leave this world without seeking your forgiveness. In hiding the Queen Stone and accusing you of its theft, the countess and I did something terribly, terribly wrong. We sought to protect our precious Rose – to steer her away from what we felt sure would be an unhappy path – but our deceit brought more unhappiness than we could possibly have imagined: 'the curse of the Queen Stone' indeed. We suffered our punishment – the loss of our beautiful daughter – but I know that you have also been cruelly punished. Your whole life has been shaped by our foolish decision – and quite unjustly. Let this, my confession, stand as evidence to clear your name and pardon you of your conviction . . .

When I look at Thomas, his face is rigid with emotion. Somewhere behind those dark-lashed eyes, he is unravelling the cruel riddle of his life. I take hold of his hand.

Then, a voice that tightens my stomach into a knot:

'What a delightful surprise!'

We look down, horrified, to see Clarence standing there by the atrium fireplace.

'Back from the grave, Agatha! Gracious – you really are an obstinate little thing, aren't you?' He raises a champagne glass to me, tips his head right back and drains it, then he allows it to fall and smash to bits on the marble floor. He starts towards us, across the atrium and up the stairs, walking slowly. He is still in the same foul, muddy clothes he was wearing when I last saw him, but now he has a peacock-green smoking jacket belted over his filthy shirt. He looks like some sort of troll, his hair wild with oil and muck. 'And so nice to see *you*, Mr Walters – though I had hoped the job at Penrith would keep you away just a little longer. How are you enjoying being paid with *Asquith* money?'

Thomas's face is cold, incredulous. 'What?'

'Well, where do you think the mysterious "donation" came from to pay your wages? A brilliant idea of mine – I saw your charming animals in the church on Christmas Day, and the minister told me they were your work. Then, after our little . . . discussion the other day –' he rubs his jaw – 'I thought I would get you out of the way for a while.'

'You—' Thomas starts, but Clarence is in full flow, swaggering up the stairs.

'And *thank you* for reading us that most entertaining tale just now. Who'd have thought it, eh? Old Uncle

Henry playing a naughty prank to stop our wild Rose from eloping with a lowly carpenter! And I have to admit to being slow about this one, Walters, old chap.' He has joined us on the landing now. Every muscle in my body tenses as the gap closes between us. 'All this time I honestly had no idea that this brat was your offspring with *Cousin Rose*! They kept that one quiet, didn't they? Our very own Romeo and Juliet! Love against all odds, and such a tragic ending.' He tuts regretfully, stopping right in front of Thomas. 'I'll tell you what *is* tragic, Walters,' and his lip curls horribly. '*I* was meant to marry pretty little Rose, so we could keep all the lovely money and property and jewels in the family.' He leers at Thomas as he spits: 'What a *pity* you got there first.'

Thomas's face has been stony all through this fiendish speech, his jaw tight with rage. At these last words, his hands shoot out and seize Clarence by the throat.

Even as his face purples, Clarence manages to purse his lips and whistle, and a booming bark answers from downstairs.

Brutus!

The monstrous dog bounds up the stairs, snarling, and Thomas throws Clarence backwards. He hits the floor, gasps and laughs hysterically.

'Oops! Down, Brutus,' he calls, catching hold of the dog's collar. The dog strains and chokes, whining to sink his teeth into Thomas's leg. 'In a minute, boy,' Clarence chortles, wrestling him back. 'You can have what *you* want, as soon as I've got what *I* want. Now, sit.'

He gets to his feet and catches his breath. His hooded, vulture eyes are burning into me. 'Give me the Queen Stone, Agatha.'

I snap the box shut and take a step back. I glance quickly down into the atrium. Where is Mr Hetherington? He is supposed to be here now, defending my right to this inheritance . . .

Bryn is sticking to my side like glue. Thomas has his arm in front of me, guarding me as Clarence advances. 'Get away from her, Asquith,' he warns.

Clarence grins. 'Heel, Brutus,' he murmurs, and the beast crawls to his side, teeth bared and ready. 'Round 'em up!' My insides cramp and go cold. The dog snaps at our legs, driving all three of us back against the shield. 'Wait, Brutus,' Clarence says softly. 'Wait . . .'

The dog's muzzle is so close to me I can feel the heat of his breath. I can't move. Clarence reaches forward very, very slowly and lifts the jewel box from my nerveless fingers. As he opens the box, his mouth opens too. Saliva drools from his mouth.

Clarence gazes at the opal for a moment, then smiles a disturbing smile and stretches up above my head to take the King Stone from its mount within the shield. 'Meet your queen,' he whispers, nestling the black opal into the silk-lined box. Side by side, they are hypnotic: King Stone and Queen Stone together in the dark-silk nest – the moon and midnight. The light from Bryn's oil lamp flickers, and bright flames dance through the opals. I can see whole worlds within them – burning galaxies of colour.

'The curse of the Queen Stone is lifted,' Clarence declares. 'As the true earl, the true heir, I will rule with *two* magnificent talismans – noble tradition and new prosperity! The baroness will come running back to me when she hears I have them *both*. The Thirtieth Earl of Gosswater will go down in the history books – my portrait will hang in galleries around the world. And all because you are *mine*.' Clarence caresses the opals lovingly, his eyes yellow in the lamp light.

'*Mine*,' I say through clenched teeth. I want justice. I want to wipe the smile off his gloating, bloated face. 'The Queen Stone is *mine*, Clarence – you can't just take it from me.'

'*Of course* I can just take it from you, Agatha. Do you have any idea how families like ours get to be so gloriously, disgustingly rich? We *take* things from other people. Taking things is what Asquiths do best!'

'My grandfather wanted *me* to have the Queen Stone,' I insist. Brutus snaps his jaws as I raise my voice. 'He said so in his will,' I hiss.

'*My grandfather?*' Clarence mocks. '*My grandfather* is dead now, so it doesn't really matter what the old buffer wanted, does it, Agatha?'

'It *does*. It was his last wish . . .'

'Oh, do shut up! You sound exactly like Hethering-ton – frightful little rat of a man. *Legal bequest* this and *moral obligation* that. Wouldn't stop going on about what the earl wanted. *I'm* the earl now, I kept saying, but he went on and on! Even after I'd told him you were most probably dead.' He laughs. 'In the end I'm afraid I had to set the hounds on him.'

'You told him Agatha was – *You did what?*' Thomas is staring, as if he is lost in the middle of a bad dream.

'Oh, I'm pretty sure he made it back to his carriage all right. But it was such fun watching him run – scampering across the grass, papers flying everywhere, and the hounds snapping at his heels – VIEW HALLOA!'

At the hunting cry, Brutus starts barking wildly, chasing around in circles after the imaginary fox.

This is my chance. I snatch the opals from Clarence's hand, snapping the box shut and clutching it to my chest as I make for the stairs. 'Thomas, Bryn – quickly!'

Clarence is laughing. 'You won't get far!'

At the foot of the stairs I stop, frozen. The front door has been left ajar – there is a crack of darkness and, through it, I can hear the baying of the hounds.

'Oh, didn't I say?' Clarence calls. 'The hounds are still loose! They must have got your scent, Agatha – they're coming for you now. *And* for your daddy, and your funny little friend. They are going to rip you all to shreds.' He is holding a brass hunting horn – the one from the table on the landing. He leans over the balustrade and blows a series of short, excited blasts. Brutus tears past us down the stairs to greet the pack; he races around the atrium, sending furniture crashing to the marble floor. The barking of the hounds is suddenly more frenzied – they are closer already – closer still – and then they are here – pouring up the front steps, thick claws scraping at the front door, which bursts open as they surge into the atrium in a great, white, yelping wave.

42

I turn and scrabble back up the stairs, my limbs useless with terror. 'What are you doing, Bryn? *This* way!'

'I'll hold the hounds back!' he shouts, going past me. 'Get away from here, Aggie! Thomas, help her!'

Thomas hauls me back up the stairs, away from Bryn and the yelping bedlam below. Clarence blows the horn again and the hounds leap and yap, crazed by the sound. The last I see of Bryn is the wave of writhing animals crashing over him, swallowing him up completely.

'NO!'

Thomas pulls me up on to the landing, but Clarence is there waiting for us. '*I'll* take those, Agatha,' he snarls, trying to wrench the opals from my grasp. He kicks my legs from beneath me and I fall flat, the box skidding away from my fingers. Thomas is wrestling Clarence to the floor: 'RUN, Aggie!' he shouts. 'Find somewhere to hide!' I grab the box and stagger to my feet, half-running, half-clambering up the next flight of stairs. There is shouting behind me, thumping and bellowing and the booming bark of Brutus, distinct above the chaos of the hounds.

As I reach the top of the staircase, I turn, hoping to see Thomas close behind me, but instead I see Clarence, crawling up the stairs on his hands and knees, his face bloodied and mad.

He is coming after me.

I stumble along the corridor, past the bedrooms, checking over my shoulder, gasping for breath. I make for the Long Gallery. I duck through the heavy curtains into the darkness – *Where can I hide?* Past the paintings – the fox hunt, the witch-burning . . . There is a table here draped with a cloth that reaches all the way to the floor – I scurry beneath it, drawing my knees up to my pounding chest. I bury my face in the skirt of my silk dress, trying to quiet my frantic breathing. *Where is Thomas? He would stop Clarence if he could . . . Is he hurt? Dead?*

There are footsteps now, slow and limping. 'Gone to ground have you, little fox?' Clarence mutters. I hear the heavy curtain drawn back and see a light burning through the blackness; he must have brought a lamp from the corridor to hunt for me. I can hear him breathing. He walks right up to the table I am hiding beneath. His filthy slippers stop for a moment, then turn and walk back again, the pool of light following his uneven steps. I wait until I can no longer hear him.

I wait a moment longer.

Then I lift the tablecloth and peer out.

'FOUND YOU!' Clarence's voice explodes in the silence and I scream with fright. As I scramble to my feet, I am aware of him lurching behind me. There is only one way to run. I head for Rose's room, hurtling through the deadly gloom of the gallery, the opals still clutched tightly in my hand.

'STOP, Agatha!' he thunders.

But I don't stop – I *won't*.

'I said STOP!'

Suddenly the shadows and the light are spinning around each other: I glance up and see Clarence's oil lamp tumbling through the air above me – it whistles past my head and smashes on the floor just before my feet. I gasp and leap as the oil whooshes up into a searing white flame. Flying and falling the final few feet to the door of Rose's room, I push the tapestry aside and grab the door handle, twisting it furiously, but it is no use – the room is locked.

Behind me, the fire is taking hold already, raging up the walls of the dry, dusty gallery, licking at the oil paint and the antique wood and the medieval tapestries, devouring centuries of Asquith heirlooms in moments. Behind the yellow-white flames I can see the dark shape of Cousin Clarence.

My breathing is shallow and panicked now – smoke burns my eyes and my throat. I try the door again, shoving all my weight against it, but it's no use. *What can I do?* A wisp of song floats into my head, soft as gossamer: Rose's lullaby. And I remember what Old Moll said: *Even when she was weak as water, she'd still get out of bed and climb up the back stairs to the nursery just to hold you and sing to you . . .* The back stairs – there must be a door here somewhere. I feel my way along the rear wall of the gallery, through hellish heat and the stench of smoke. My hands are flat against the panelling, feeling up and down, until at last they find something – a cold metal catch beneath my thumb. I look around for Clarence, but all I can see is thick, grey smoke; all I can hear is the roaring of the fire as it rips through the Long Gallery. I click the catch, open the door and slip through, closing it quickly behind me and gasping at the clean air.

A dark, narrow stairwell. The howl of a hound echoes from the ground floor, and I know I must go up, just as Rose did. *She was found there on the staircase one morning – cold as stone. She'd been tryin' to come to you one last time.*

A noise from just below me. Did Clarence see me come through that door?

I must keep moving.

Up, up, up I go.

Up past the nursery, the servants' rooms, the attics, up until I cannot go any further. Here at the top there is a small, white door.

I draw the rusty bolt, push the door open and step through – out on to the vast, sloping rooftops of Goss-water Hall.

43

The wind whips my breath away — bitter and wintry, it buffets me so hard I have to lean into it to stay upright. Columns of smoke are pouring from the windows below and the wind tears at the smoke and flames so that the whole night is burning. There is a sound, somewhere amidst the roar of the wind and fire — a ragged calling in the air. Dark shapes are flapping blackly around me. At first I think they are the evil spirits I saw circling Sexton Black like a dark halo. But then I realize that they are not spirits at all — they are living creatures. *Ravens.*

They soar so close to me I can see the gleam of their liquid-black eyes, the sheen of each long feather. They stretch out their huge black-fingered wings and caw — airborne witches shrieking their curses. Then they bank and turn – flocking away from the house, out towards the lake and the western fells – a shimmering ribbon of darkness. And then they are gone.

Clarence bragged that he had lifted the curse of the Queen Stone, but now his house is burning and the ravens have flown. *When the ravens fly, the roof will fall and every Asquith of Gosswater Hall . . .*

'AGATHA!' A voice behind me. Clarence emerges from the little door, hunched like an ape. He crawls across the rooftop. 'Where are you going now, little cousin? There is nowhere else to run to! Unless you want to *fly?*'

I shuffle backwards, closer to the edge of the roof. I am still clasping the box of opals; my other hand grips the weathered head of a gargoyle. The wind gusts violently and the world below swirls like a whirlpool. Somewhere down there, through the blackness and the flames and the smoke, lies the moat that surrounds Gosswater Hall . . . Could I make it?

No, Aggie – you'd miss the moat and smash to pieces. And even if you did land in the water, you'd still break every bone in your body.

'Give me the box, Agatha. Give me my OPALS!' In the ghastly light of the flames, I see Clarence's face, streaked with soot and blood, his eyes burning with greed. He would push me off this roof in an instant if it weren't for the jewels in my hand. 'Give. Them. To. ME . . .'

I grip the handle of the jewel case more tightly: 'I'd rather die.'

His voice softens: 'Oh, that can be arranged, Agatha . . .'

The wind roars, the smoke billows, Clarence creeps closer, closer . . .

Then another voice: 'Get AWAY from her, Asquith.'

Thomas! It's Thomas!

'GET AWAY FROM MY DAUGHTER.'

Thomas is leaping across the roof towards us. Clarence has less than a second to decide what he will do, and I see the decision flicker in his eyes like a cold flame. He makes a lunge for the opals and I dive to one side, but the slates slide away and I lose my footing. I hear the crunch of knuckles hitting bone – and Clarence squeals. There is a blur of noise and pain – I am slipping over the edge of the rooftop, screaming, scrabbling for something to hold on to, then a strong hand catches mine and I gasp as my body jolts back against the wall. My toes find a narrow ledge and I look up to see Thomas's face above me.

'I've got you, Aggie. Give me your other hand.'

'I can't.'

He sees that I am still, somehow, clutching the box of opals. 'Let them go.'

My fingers are clamped around the handle, stubborn as stone.

'They're just *things*, Aggie!'

'They're *mine*,' I sob. The narrow ledge is crumbling under my weight.

Thomas grips my hand tighter, his eyes shining with tears. 'And *you* are *mine*, and I've only just found you. I'm not losing you now. Give me your hand.'

All by themselves, my fingers loosen and the box simply drops away into the gloom.

Clarence's hideous face looms over the edge of the roof, just inches away from us: 'NOOO!' he yells, reaching wildly for the jewels; the guttering cracks and gives way, and Clarence suddenly lurches forward, plunging down into the blackness.

A long scream, a sickening thud, a splash.

And he has gone.

Thomas grasps my other hand and pulls me up on to the rooftop. I am sobbing, my whole body shaking with fear. Thomas wraps his arms around me tightly – it is the first time he has ever held me.

'It's all right, bairn,' he says. 'Cush now. I've got you.' It is the same gentle voice he uses for the animals. I press my face against him and the cold wind blows around us. My hand that clung so desperately to the opals feels aching and empty. *They are gone – the King Stone and the Queen Stone. Both lost.* Thomas holds me and strokes my hair and wipes the tears from my face. He takes my trembling hand in his – strong and warm and safe.

And it doesn't feel empty any more.

44

The journey back down the servants' staircase is a long, dark spiral of smoke. Thomas leads me quickly down and I hold my scarf over my face, coughing and coughing. Once we pass the first floor, it is easier to breathe. At last we fall through the door into the kitchens and stumble out through the laundry into the tradesman's yard. The clean night air is the sweetest thing I have ever tasted. We gulp and splutter and rub our eyes.

Above us, Gosswater Hall is burning. The house groans like a dying beast. Windows shatter and smoke churns out, billowing like storm clouds, heavy with ash.

'Bryn,' I say. 'Where's Bryn?'

'I don't know.' Thomas shakes his head. 'He was

there on the stairs—'

'And then the hounds came.' I look around for them, listening for their yapping and baying.

'No, *after* the hounds came – when I was fightin' Clarence. Bryn got that giant dog off me . . .' Thomas's hand goes to his thigh and I see his clothes are ripped and soaked red with blood.

'Thomas – you're hurt!'

'It'll keep till we get home, lass. I can walk.'

'But what happened to Bryn?'

'I'm sorry,' Thomas says. 'I didn't see him again.'

There is a grim moment of silence. The wind drops, and an icy shiver bites its way down my spine. I imagine my friend – sprawled on the atrium floor, his limbs savaged, fresh blood in his fox-red hair.

'Bryn! Bryn!' We go around the building to the front of the house, running and coughing and calling his name. 'BRYN!'

Then I see him – in the grass on the other side of the moat. He is lying there on the ground, just a lifeless shape beside a large patch of snow.

'Bryn?' I stop and Thomas stops too.

'I'll go,' he says.

But then Bryn moves – he sits up and turns to face us. He puts a finger to his lips, and beckons us over. We cross the bridge and driveway, and tread slowly through the wet grass.

A few paces nearer and I stop again, blinking. The

patch of snow is not a patch of snow at all. It is the hounds. All of them – forty, at least – lying down quietly, docile as lapdogs.

'Bryn? How did you—'

'I told you I'm good wi' animals.' He grins, getting up. There is not a scratch on him.

Brutus is there too. He sniffs the air as Thomas and I approach, and he whines. Bryn frowns at him and the beast buries his muzzle between his huge paws.

Bryn holds his arms out and I hug him tightly. He is safe. Somehow, we are all safe.

'Are you all right, Aggie?' Bryn asks. 'What happened to Clarence?'

As Thomas explains what happened on the rooftop, I see my cousin's face in my mind, the second before he fell – bloodied, bloated, blank – and I almost feel sorry. There was no man left behind those vulture eyes: greed had hollowed him out. If his ghost ever rises from its grave, I know it will be one of those bat-winged spirits that whirls like a wicked wind about Sexton Black.

'And the opals?' Bryn asks.

I shake my head. 'Gone.'

I look back at the flaming building behind me. My throat burns. I don't know what I am feeling now – grief? Release?

There is a thunderous sigh, and the upper part of the north wing collapses into the moat. Soon Gosswater Hall will be nothing but a pile of blackened stone.

'It's all gone,' I breathe.

We go home to Thomas's cottage in his cart. Once George is safely in his stable, and Thomas has cleaned and dressed the wounds on his leg, we sit down together by the fire in the parlour. Bryn dozes in his chair, exhausted. There is so much to be said between me and Thomas that neither of us knows where to start, so we say nothing for some time. Thomas has placed his letter from the late earl on the mantel above the fire. He glances up at it once, twice, as if he is wondering whether or not to burn it. At last he reaches for it, unfolds it, and reads it quietly to himself. I watch his eyes move over the words time and time again.

'Your grandfather talks of unjust punishment,' he says at last, in a low, low voice. 'But he had no idea how bad those years were . . .'

'In prison?'

'Aye. And everythin' else too. My old dad was so ashamed when I was locked up that he never spoke another word to me. Dropped down dead before I got out. I came home to find the place a near ruin, the geese wanderin' wild. Took me a long time to put it all back together – the farm, everythin' . . .' He presses his hands to his eyes. 'The worst of it all was not knowing what had happened to my Rose. Years goin' by and no word from her . . .'

'No one told you she had died?'

He shakes his head. 'I thought she must have married someone else. The very heart of me rotted away in that place.'

He stares back down at the letter. Then he takes a shaking breath and passes it to me. 'You ought to read the last bit for yourself, lass. It's about you.'

About me? I take a big breath and look at the final paragraph. This is what Grandfather's dying eyes wanted so much to say:

In reconciliation with your daughter, Agatha, I pray that you will find peace and happiness. As the child grew to resemble her mother more every day, she became a greater torment to me and to the late countess: a constant reminder of what we had done and all we had lost. I deeply regret that we were not better parents to her and that the years of her childhood have been so sadly blighted. Please love her, Mr Walters. She deserves to be loved.

I look up at Thomas through a blur of tears and see that he is crying too.

'It's not too late, is it, Aggie?' he whispers. 'To have some years that aren't sadly blighted?'

'It's not too late. For either of us.'

I give him back the letter and he grips my hand tightly. We sit there together. The wind blows outside and the fire crackles.

'I think,' I say after a while, 'I'd like to write to Miss McCarthy.'

'To Maud?'

I nod. 'Before she was sent away, she promised me that I would be all right. I thought she was just trying to make me feel better, but now I see . . . She knew I was coming home to you.'

Thomas brushes a tear roughly from his cheek. 'Aye lass,' he says. 'You write and tell her you're all right.' He squeezes my hand again and smiles that gentle, twinkling smile. 'You're all right now.'

So many terrible things have happened, so much has been lost – and yet somehow, this feels like a beginning rather than an ending. We drink hot tea. We poke the fire until it sparks and flares. We add more logs.

The cold and the darkness are not welcome here.

45

It is not until the morning that we realize Susan is missing. Thomas goes out to feed the geese and when he comes back in, his face is pale.

'Perhaps Fox has got her at last.'

We search the garden for feathers, blood in the snow, signs of a scuffle. Susan wouldn't have gone without a fight. We scour every corner of the farm. Bryn crawls through the undergrowth and I wade out into the icy water, calling for her.

We search all morning, but we find nothing. At last we give up.

'I should go back to the Hall,' Bryn says. 'I'm sorry. I've got to collect my boat. I need t' make sure the hounds are all right too, and that big stupid mutt. Check someone is lookin' after 'em.'

'I'll run you there in the cart,' Thomas says. 'Least I can do to thank you for everythin' you've done.' He looks Bryn up and down, 'Is that my old coat you're wearin'?'

Bryn blushes. 'Aye – sorry. I borrowed it last night.'

'You keep it, lad. It looks well on you.' And he pats Bryn on the shoulder.

They walk up to the yard side by side. 'You get the pony ready and I'll hitch the cart,' Thomas says.

An idea appears in my head – suddenly I know.

'Thomas – when you got home yesterday, before you came to Gosswater Hall, did you feed the geese?'

'Aye, just before I came to find you.'

I smile slowly. I am thinking of Boxing Day, when Susan escaped and ran towards us down the track. I am thinking of the time she followed Thomas halfway to Penrith . . .

'I think I know where she is.'

I am not quite prepared for the devastation we find when we get to Gosswater Hall. Smoke hangs in the frosty air like fog – bitter and black – and through the dark wisps we can just make out the skeleton of the house. Earlier this morning, Gosswater Hall was a nightmare dissolved by daylight, but now it is real again, right here in front of my eyes – a dark, smoking phantom of my past.

Something has changed within me, though. When I

let go of the opals last night, I let go of so many other things too. I think about what Bryn said, that night on the fells: *The past can tell you where you've come from, right enough, but it can't tell you who you are. Who you are is up to you right now.* And, with Bryn and Thomas by my side, I know exactly who I am. I am Aggie. And I am not here to pick a fight with the past; I am here to find a missing goose.

We leave George and the cart a safe distance away from the smoke, and walk across the grass.

'You think she followed me all the way here last night, Aggie?'

'I'm sure she did.'

And then we see her – a flash of white wings in the reeds beside the moat.

'What is she doing? Is she hurt?'

Susan is nuzzling at something beneath her. She fusses about, raises her wings awkwardly and settles herself in the reeds. I know she has seen us. Usually she would come running to Thomas, but she is not moving.

'Sue?' Thomas tiptoes towards her, holding out his hand. Susan looks up at him and clacks her black-tipped beak, but still she will not move.

'Are you hurt, Sue? Let me see.' Thomas runs his hand along her neck, he gently unfolds each wing, looking for an injury. He tucks an arm right around her to lift her up and she protests, flapping and honking. 'It's all right, Sue. Does it hurt? Cush now, girl.' He calms her and lifts her from the ground, and it is then that we understand – Susan is not hurt at all. She is guarding her nest.

Here in the snowy reeds beside the smoking ruins of Gosswater Hall, Susan has woven sticks and dead grass into a perfect oval. She has lined her nest with fluff and feathers and soft, dry leaves. In the centre of her nest, there are three large goose eggs. One of them is black. We look closer. We blink.

One large goose egg.

And two large opals.

My mouth drops open. I stretch my hand towards the opals, but Susan won't let me near.

Thomas turns to Bryn. 'Check in the pockets of that coat, will you, lad? Should be a handful o' grain in there.'

Bryn puts both hands in his pockets and his face changes. He pulls out a handful of grain in one hand, and a handful of jewels in the other.

46

My grandfather wanted me to have a nest egg – the countess's jewels – and he wanted me to be the keeper of the Queen Stone too. The opals belong together; I don't know what their destiny is, but I know I must keep them safe for now. The jewels I have plans for. Wise and kind plans . . .

'What'll happen to Gosswater Hall now? What'll happen to the hounds?' Bryn asks as Thomas and I climb into the cart.

'There will be someone else,' I say. 'Another Asquith will crawl out of the woodwork – a third cousin or something. He'll salvage what he can from the ruins of the Hall. He'll rebuild it, probably, or sell it. He'll want the hounds, I'm sure – and the horses and carriages and boats.'

Bryn nods. 'I saw a light at the gamekeeper's cottage,' he says. 'I'll go and have a word, and meet you back at the cottage in a while – if that's all right?'

'O' course it's all right, Bryn,' Thomas says. 'You're welcome at the cottage. To live there, I mean, along with me and Aggie.' He nods towards George the pony and the grumpy goose tucked under his arm. 'An' these two as well.'

Bryn opens his mouth to speak, but his eyes are filling with tears and he doesn't trust himself to say anything.

'I'm not havin' you go back to that island,' Thomas says gently. 'The cottage is your home now, lad.'

Home.

With Gosswater Hall crumbling to dust behind us, we rattle along the driveway in the cart. The afternoon is already darkening, and I am reminded of that first journey to Thomas's cottage. How angry we both were, how frightened. I look at Thomas now and he smiles back at me. Somehow, he is managing to drive with Susan tucked beneath his arm. She chatters every now and then, fussing at Thomas's coat to make sure her egg is safe in his pocket.

I find myself patting my own pockets, and my heart thrills when I feel the round shapes of the opals, the clinking tangle of jewellery. I tell Thomas about my plans for the jewels – to pay his debts and his bills, to repair the farm buildings, to put some by so that he'll never have to worry in the future . . .

'Thank you, lass,' Thomas says, swallowing hard.

'It's not Asquith money,' I say. 'It's mine. Ours.'

He nods. 'Aye. And what about *your* future, Aggie? What do you want to do?'

'So many things,' I say.

He nods again and smiles. 'That's good, bairn.'

'To start with, I would like to learn how to cook bacon so that it tastes like bacon.'

He laughs out loud, and I laugh too.

'I'd like to take Bryn to a theatre,' I say. 'He really liked the sound of *Hamlet*.' I think for a moment longer. 'And I would like to learn how to sail.' I am remembering that morning in Ivy's skiff: the rush of air, the icy spray, soaring over the water – like flying, like freedom. *Yes. That's what I want my future to feel like.*

When we get home, we don't go into the house straight away – we check on the geese first. They bustle around us in the shed, prattling and honking. Thomas places Susan's egg carefully in the straw and she settles down on it, broody and serious.

Thomas shakes his head, bewildered. 'Hasn't laid an egg since I can't remember when,' he says. 'Reckon I'll let her hatch this one.'

I nod, smoothing the feathers on top of her hard head; she hisses as me, but I don't think she means it quite like she used to.

'Susan was your mother's favourite,' Thomas says quietly. 'Funny little gosling, she was – used to follow Rose all around the garden and sleep on her lap. That was the summer we met – when I started work at the Hall.'

I think of the night I curled up in the straw with the geese, and woke to find Rose by my side. *The Ghost Girl and the goose girl.* I wonder if she will come again tonight. I wonder if she will ever come again.

After dinner, when Bryn has gone up to bed and it is just me and Thomas sitting by the fire, I tell him about the Ghost Girl. I pick my words carefully, like footsteps through fresh snow. I don't want him to think this is a child's fairy story; I know what Rose means to him.

When I tell him about the night of the storm, he nods, his eyes sparkling in the firelight.

'Did you see her at the window?'

'No. But I think perhaps . . . I *felt* her there.'

I tell him what I would like to do and he agrees, though his face is rigid and he is gripping his knees tightly. As the clock approaches midnight, we take a lantern and blankets and we make our way down to the bottom of the garden. There is a path of moonlight shimmering on the dark lake, and we head towards it.

'Looks like you could walk along it,' Thomas says in a hushed voice. 'Right across the water, all the way to Skelter Island.' He looks at me, his face drawn and pale. 'Do you think she'll come?'

'I don't know.'

We sit down together on a thick blanket and I wrap another warmly over our legs.

We gaze out at the starlit lake.

'The first thing I did when I found out what had happened,' Thomas says, 'was to row over to the island to see her tomb. I wouldn't let myself believe she was gone until I saw her name there . . .'

'You carved that rose on the silver birch,' I whisper.

'Aye. That were me.' He smiles sadly. 'She always used to say that Asquith motto was about the two of us – *for ever faithful*.' He takes a trembling breath.

With every little thing he shares with me, Rose becomes more real. I may not remember her, but I feel as if I know her now. And I know that she will always be part of me: part of the person I have chosen to become.

'I'd like to go there with you,' I say. 'To Rose's tomb. We'll take flowers.'

Thomas nods, his face crumpling with tears. 'Snow-drops,' he whispers hoarsely. 'We'll take the first snowdrops o' the year.'

'The first snowdrops of the century.' I smile, feeling that aching in my throat. Warm tears spill down my cheeks. 'And we'll take roses in the summer – armfuls of wild roses.'

'Aye.'

303

I take his hand and he puts his arm around my shoulder, squeezing me tightly against his side. He kisses the top of my head. *My dad.* I try the word out in my head before I dare to say it out loud.

'She's here with us,' I whisper. The darkness around us is somehow less dark – we are cocooned in a warm, white light – pale as pearls, soft as silk. Cool, feather-white fingers touch my face, my hand.

'Aye,' he gasps, 'my Rose.'

Her arms are around us both – her true-love and her child: a family.

'Is she sayin' goodbye?' he breathes.

'I think so.'

She is happy now – we are together, and we are safe. The secrets of the past are secrets no longer: she can rest peacefully at last.

We watch her go – a wisp of opal-white light, following the moonlit path across the lake towards the island. She soars and circles like a swift, higher and higher, embracing the infinite sky. *So happy.*

Then she glitters into a silvery mist that dances with the darkness, and dissolves.

She is a million shining stars.

NOTES AND ACKNOWLEDGEMENTS

The Ghost of Gosswater was inspired by the breathtaking landscape of the Lake District and by the works of some of my favourite writers: Emily and Charlotte Brontë, Daphne du Maurier, Robert Louis Stevenson, Frances Hodgson Burnett and Arthur Ransome to name a few. Shakespeare's *Hamlet* also played a significant part – with ghosts and vengeance, truth and uncertainty being so much at its heart. Gosswater itself is a fictional place, loosely based on Ullswater (about ten miles away from the town of Penrith).

This book was rewritten, edited and completed during the COVID-19 Lockdown of spring 2020, so huge, heartfelt thanks to my wonderful partner James, not only for supporting and encouraging me with my writing, but also for some top-notch, in-at-the-deep-end dadding of our very lively toddler: I couldn't have done this without you, my darling.

Thank you to Fred, the aforementioned lively toddler, for being a source of so much joy and laughter (and for being a fairly reliable afternoon napper), and – I'm sure I speak for many locked-down parents here – THANK YOU to the creators of *Peppa Pig*.

Enormous thanks as always to my magnificent publisher, Chicken House, and to all the fabulous, hard-working Chickens who helped to incubate and hatch this book: Barry, Elinor, Rachel H, Jazz, Esther,

Kesia, Sarah, Laura and Lucy. Extra special thanks of course to the wonder that is Rachel Leyshon, an editor par excellence; never has such patience, wisdom, tact and kindness been so deeply appreciated by an author.

Thank you to the immensely talented Helen Crawford-White for another stunning (and spooky!) cover design. And to the eagle-eyed Daphne for her brilliant copy-editing – the devil is in the detail!

Thank you to my adored agent Luigi – your support and encouragement helped me to get this book finished when I thought it was impossible. I am so glad to be part of the LBA family (and to feel like an honorary Bonomi too).

The school I have taught at since 2015 very kindly allowed me to take a sabbatical so that I might focus exclusively on writing, and this book would not have been finished without that precious time. So thank you, Kent College, Canterbury. Thanks specifically to friend and KC colleague Martin Cox for being my sailing consultant and teaching me about the reality of tacking! Thank you and farewell to KC's Dr Gerald Colson – a dedicated, kind-hearted and accomplished gentleman who was always so supportive of my writing, and who sadly passed away just before this book was finished.

Love and thanks to all my dear pals – writers, teachers, mums and publishing folk – for keeping me sane and cheerful.

Big, grateful hugs to my wonderful parents Mary and Rick Strange, my brothers Will and Pete, and to the Barbers too, for all your love and support, and for helping so much with our beautiful boy.

Congratulations to Daniel Jack Tully and Grace Amos who won the competition to have their family names featured in *The Ghost of Gosswater* (page 266!) and well done to all the brilliant bookworms who were nominated by their parents and teachers: Freddie Hooker; Lola Weiss; Archie Aitchison; Shivani, Rishi and Rohini Kaushik, and the awesome Book Brothers. Hurrah for the fabulous booktuber Gavin Hetherington (aka @theGavGav7) whose name was already – somewhat eerily – included in the book.

Thank you to ALL the amazing booksellers, book bloggers, librarians, teachers, reviewers and Twitterers for spreading the word and for believing so passionately that good children's books can change the world – because they really can.

A mother's love is at the heart of this story, and I would like to make a special mention of one particular mother (and book lover) here: Helen Harflett. Her daughter, Esther, tells me that this book would have been just her cup of tea, so it is only right that Helen should be remembered within its pages.

Lastly, thankYOU, dear reader, for choosing to read *The Ghost of Gosswater* and for joining Aggie on this adventure – I sincerely hope you enjoyed it. Follow me on Twitter @TheLucyStrange for news, giveaways, and updates on what is coming next . . .

ALSO BY LUCY STRANGE

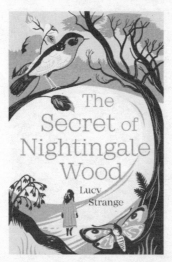

THE SECRET OF NIGHTINGALE WOOD

Something terrible has happened in the Abbott family and nobody is talking about it.

Mama is ill. Father has taken a job abroad. Nanny Jane is too busy looking after baby Piglet to pay any attention to Henrietta and the things she sees – or thinks she sees – in the shadows of their new home, Hope House.

All alone, with only stories for company, Henry discovers that Hope House is full of strange secrets: a forgotten attic, thick with cobwebs; ghostly figures glimpsed through dusty windows; mysterious firelight that flickers in the trees beyond the garden.

One night she ventures into the darkness of Nightingale Wood. What she finds there will change her whole world . . .

'Superbly balanced between readability and poetry [. . .] this is an assured debut.'
GUARDIAN

'Perfect in so many ways!'
EMMA CARROLL

Paperback, ISBN 978-1-910655-03-0, £6.99 • ebook, ISBN 978-1-910655-63-4, £6.99

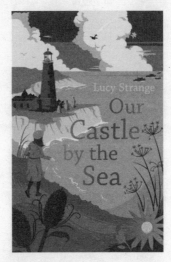

OUR CASTLE BY THE SEA

England is at war. Growing up in a lighthouse, twelve-year-old Pet's world has been one of storms, secret tunnels and stories about sea monsters. But now the clifftops are a terrifying battleground, and her family is torn apart. This is the story of a girl who is small, afraid and unnoticed. A girl who freezes with fear at the enemy planes ripping through the skies overhead. A girl who is somehow destined to become part of the strange, ancient legend of the Daughters of Stone . . .

'A beautiful story.'
KIRAN MILLWOOD HARGRAVE

'This mesmerising novel is as much
fairy tale as historical fiction.'
THE TELEGRAPH

Paperback, ISBN 978-1-911077-83-1, £6.99 • ebook, ISBN 978-1-911490-52-4, £6.99